Eric still had her by the waist where he'd grabbed her just as the car whooshed past them, spewing exhaust and burning rubber into the air.

Christina had stumbled back against Eric's chest, and he pulled her tightly against his body. "Are you okay?"

"That was close." Her voice shook and she cleared her throat. "What's the matter with that guy? Didn't he see us?"

"He saw us, Christina."

Her heart pounded in her chest and her breath came out in short spurts. "That's crazy. We're the FBI, for God's sake."

He held out his hand. "Do you want me to drive? Your hands are trembling."

She dropped the keys into his palm without a word. If he wanted to play the big, strong protector, who was she to argue?

THE DISTRICT

—

CAROL ERICSON

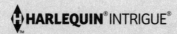

Recycling programs
for this product may
not exist in your area.

For Deputy Chief Greg Huber,
one of my many go-to guys for research

ISBN-13: 978-0-373-69759-5

THE DISTRICT

Copyright © 2014 by Carol Ericson

Printed in U.S.A.

ABOUT THE AUTHOR

Carol Ericson lives with her husband and two sons in Southern California, home of state-of-the-art cosmetic surgery, wild freeway chases, palm trees bending in the Santa Ana winds and a million amazing stories. These stories, along with hordes of virile men and feisty women, clamor for release from Carol's head. It makes for some interesting headaches until she sets them free to fulfill their destinies and her readers' fantasies. To find out more about Carol, her books and her strange headaches, please visit her website, www.carolericson.com, "Where romance flirts with danger."

Books by Carol Ericson

HARLEQUIN INTRIGUE
1034—THE STRANGER AND I
1079—A DOCTOR-NURSE ENCOUNTER
1117—CIRCUMSTANTIAL MEMORIES
1184—THE SHERIFF OF SILVERHILL
1231—THE McCLINTOCK PROPOSAL
1250—A SILVERHILL CHRISTMAS
1267—NAVY SEAL SECURITY*
1273—MOUNTAIN RANGER RECON*
1320—TOP GUN GUARDIAN*
1326—GREEN BERET BODYGUARD*
1349—OBSESSION‡
1355—EYEWITNESS‡
1373—INTUITION‡
1379—DECEPTION‡
1409—RUN, HIDE**
1415—CONCEAL, PROTECT**
1450—TRAP, SECURE**
1458—CATCH, RELEASE**
1487—THE BRIDGEΔ
1492—THE DISTRICTΔ

*Brothers in Arms
‡Guardians of Coral Cove
**Brothers in Arms: Fully Engaged
ΔBrody Law

CAST OF CHARACTERS

Eric Brody—An FBI agent investigating a serial killer, he brings a lot of baggage to his job, including his kidnapping as a child and the suspicions surrounding his father. He may be strong enough to overcome all of that, but is he strong enough to work alongside his ex-fiancée without falling under her spell again?

Christina Sandoval—She's landed her dream assignment of working with the FBI's serial killer unit, but the dream may become a nightmare when her current investigation brings her ex-fiancé and the father of her child back into her life...especially since Eric doesn't know he's a father.

Kendall Brody—The toddler daughter of Christina and Eric might possess powers stronger than Christina's own, but Christina has no intention of finding out how much more powerful.

Octavio Sandoval—Christina's father is a *brujo,* but are his powers enough to save her, or will they be the instrument of her demise?

Vivi Sandoval—Christina's half sister is more involved in the witchcraft of their heritage than Christina, and when she goes into hiding from a killer she urges Christina to do the same.

Libby Rivers—The owner of an occult bookshop in the Haight-Ashbury district, she may know more about the killer than she's willing to share.

Nigel Ashford—An old hippie and denizen of the Haight-Ashbury district, he inhabits the perimeter of the occult world. But will he do anything, including murder, to be a full-fledged member?

Darius Cole—Vivi's friend is worried about her and is desperately trying to find her, but if Vivi doesn't trust him, why should Christina?

Liz Fielding—The serial killer's first victim has a strange connection to Eric Brody's kidnapping as a child, which makes Eric believe the trauma of his past is connected to his current case.

Marie Giardano—The SFPD records keeper has seen a lot in her thirty-five years with the department and she has her own suspicions about the Brody tragedy, but she's afraid to share them.

Chapter One

Nine times out of ten a dead body will win a staring contest.

Christina blinked and looked away from the lifeless eyes of the twentysomething vic, a gruesome slash across her throat, a tarot card shoved between her stiff fingers.

Tarot cards—Christina knew a thing or two about them. She would've expected death on his white horse in this case, but the killer had left the maiden and the lion, an indicator of strength.

Her gaze shifted away from the body and skimmed the trees, their leaves rustling with impatience. "Has anyone checked the surrounding area yet?"

Lieutenant Fitch with the San Francisco P.D. waved his pale hand. "You go right ahead, Agent Sandoval."

She ground her back teeth together, adjusted her shoulder holster and tromped toward the tree line. If not for that tarot card, she wouldn't even be here.

The dense nature preserve enveloped her in a cool embrace, muting the voices of the crime scene investigators in the trail behind her. The weak San Francisco sun, still shrugging off the fog, penetrated the foliage in wisps and strands, throwing a beam of light here and dappled shadows there.

She inhaled the scent of eucalyptus, which cleared her senses and ramped up her adrenaline. The murder victim had been jogging on the trail either early this morning or sometime last night. The predator had surprised her, flying at her like an animal on the prowl—lying in wait.

Her nostrils flared and she scanned the underbrush. Lying in wait. He must've been watching, waiting for his prey.

Hunching forward, she crept farther into the darkness, her footfalls silenced by nature's carpet beneath her, the strands of a willow brushing her face. She veered to the right, aligning herself with the body on the trail.

She cranked her head over her shoulder and detected flashes of color and movement from the cops and techs milling around the vic. He could've seen her coming from here, but would've had no time to prepare his attack.

She looked up. A live oak tree towered a few feet in front of her. She approached it, studying the ground around the base of the trunk. Something had disturbed the leaves layered on the dirt, but plenty of creatures roamed this area—not just the two-legged, deadly kind.

She reached out, running her hand down the rough bark that scratched her fingers. Here and there she traced smooth areas of the trunk where pieces of bark had broken away from the old tree.

Stretching her arms out, she wedged her palms against the tree trunk and hung her head between her arms. She closed her eyes.

The subtle sounds of nature came to life—the rustle of a bird's wings, the creak of a branch, the scurrying of an insect across a log.

And then it slammed into her chest. The evil. She felt it like a palpable curtain dropping around her, smothering her. He'd been here.

She jerked her head up, her eyes narrowing. She shed her jacket and secured her weapon in her holster. The bark of the tree chaffed her palms as she grabbed the first branch with both hands. She hoisted herself up and planted the rubber soles of her practical shoes against the trunk. Walking up the tree trunk, she lunged for the next branch and then swung her legs over the side of it.

Straddling the branch, she could just see over the top of the lower bushes and trees that bordered the jogging trail. She pulled herself into a crouch and reached for the next branch that curved against the trunk—a natural seat, a window on the world.

She nestled her back against the trunk, her legs hanging over the side of the branch. Lieutenant Fitch came into view, pointing and gesturing with his hands—which she'd noticed before were sprinkled with red hair—basically running the show.

Farther down the trail a clutch of people crowded against the yellow police tape, all leaning toward the crime scene like magnets drawn to some irresistible force.

She got it. The same morbid curiosity had propelled her into a job with a special serial killer unit within the FBI. She'd been fascinated with these crimes ever since she'd followed the Phone Book Killer case at the tender age of twelve.

She shivered—that fascination, along with an uncanny ability to empathize with both the killers and their victims, drove her to this work. She didn't really empathize with the killers, but for some reason she could tune in to their thought processes. Not that she'd ever told anyone that before—anyone but Eric.

And that had been a colossal mistake.

She sat up straighter on the branch and peered at the trail beyond the spectators. He would've seen her coming from this vantage point. Would've been able to jump from his lookout post and intercept her on the trail, introducing her to the sharp edge of his knife.

She took a deep breath. Was that artificial smell among the natural elements cologne? Tobacco?

She reached for the branch above her to lean forward and scope out the ground. Her fingers collided with the smooth edge of a card. She snatched her hand away, curled one leg beneath her and slowly rose from her seated position.

Someone had shoved another tarot card in the crack of some mottled bark. She pulled a tissue from her pocket. Pinching the card between two tissue-covered fingers, she plucked it from its hiding place. She turned the card over.

The fool.

Her nerve endings buzzed with curiosity and excitement. Again, she would've expected the death card. Instead, he'd left the card for strength and the fool.

Had this tarot card been at the two other crime scenes and they'd missed it? What was he trying to tell them?

She huffed out a breath. If her mother had allowed her to continue down the path her father wanted to carve for her, she'd probably understand this killer's message.

Christina pulled an evidence baggie from her pocket and dropped the card inside. She scanned her perch for anything else the killer may have left behind—threads, hair, more tarot cards.

Nothing jumped out at her, not even those vague feelings that sometimes insinuated themselves into her psyche. Once she'd found the killer's perch, she'd readied herself for a rush of feelings, feelings that often made her nauseous. This time she'd only experienced the taste of evil at the base of the tree.

She brushed away the trickle of sweat at her hairline and lowered herself back to the ground. She swept her jacket up from the carpet of mulch and froze.

A twig cracked again.

She jerked her head in the direction of the sound. Her gaze darted between the branches and leaves of the dense foliage. She held her breath. The entire park held its breath, too, waiting for someone to make a move.

"Agent Sandoval?"

The interloper crashing through the trees behind her set the forest in motion. Birds took flight, scattering leaves in their haste. A squirrel scurried up the tree trunk, pausing to blink at her with its bright, challenging eyes. The trees took up their groaning and creaking once more.

Christina turned, holding out her hands, palms up. "Careful there, cowboy. I've probably already done enough damage here."

"Ma'am?" The officer cocked his head, looking all of twelve.

"Call me Christina." She pinched the evidence baggie between two fingers and wiggled it in front of her. "Another tarot card. I think our killer scoped out the victim from this tree."

The cop's mouth dropped open as he took a step back. "I'll get the lieutenant and have him send the CSI guys out here. Did you find anything else?"

"Nope, just the card." And one helluva creepy feeling. Somehow she knew Lieutenant Fitch would dismiss any and all creepy feelings, so she'd keep them to herself. She always did.

She followed the broad blue-clad back through the trees, back to the running trail. The young cop was already hopping from foot to foot in front of Lieutenant Fitch and gesturing with his hands.

Fitch gazed over his officer's shoulder and narrowed his eyes as Christina emerged into the clearing. Did he think she'd planted the evidence? As FBI, she'd worked with resentful detectives before, and Fitch seemed to be taking his place among them.

If she hadn't already been here due to the previous tarot

card murder, Fitch probably wouldn't have bothered contacting the FBI about this one.

She plastered on her sweetest smile and waved the plastic bag. "How about that, Lieutenant? Looks like our boy stationed himself in one tall tree, staking out his next victim."

"Let me see that." He snapped his fingers and held out his hand.

She dropped the evidence baggie into his palm. "Another tarot card—the fool this time. Those cards mean something to him. He's leaving us a message."

The cop swallowed, his Adam's apple bobbing in his thin neck. "Maybe he's a fortune-teller?"

Fitch practically growled at him. "Go get some more yellow tape and tell CSI the crime scene's just been extended."

Christina called after the hunched shoulders. "You might be on to something, Officer."

The lieutenant snapped his reddish brows together. "Don't encourage him. He's just a rookie on patrol. I can assure you, Agent Sandoval, you're not dealing with some hick department."

"This is San Francisco. I never thought I was, Lieutenant." She turned her head and covered her mouth with her hand. Inferiority complex much? "Can you tell me anything more about the murder?"

"Without an autopsy, it's what we suspected at first—severe head trauma followed by the slitting of the throat."

"Blunt object?"

"Yep."

"He must be incapacitating them with the blow to the head, which then allows him to cut their throats."

"Victim lost a lot of blood."

"Just like Liz Fielding and the one up in Portland."

"At least he's consistent."

"Except for this." She flicked the bag he still held in

his hand. "Unless we missed something at those other crime scenes."

"Is this going to send you back up to Portland, Agent Sandoval?"

She tossed her ponytail over one shoulder. "Why? Trying to get rid of me, Lieutenant Fitch?"

"Naw, we love it when the fibbies come around and trample all over our procedures and protocol."

Arching one eyebrow, she said, "Is that what you think I'm doing?"

"You're all right, so far, Agent Sandoval. We've just had a few bad experiences with you boys…ah, folks."

"You can start by calling me Christina, and I'm not here to trample over your procedures and protocol. I'm here to find a killer and get some justice for these victims. I hope that's your objective, too, Lieutenant Fitch."

He thrust out his hand. "Call me Charlie."

"Done deal, Charlie. Now let's nail this SOB."

"I MISS YOU, Kendall. Be a good girl for G-Ma." Christina blew kisses at the laptop until her mother's face filled the screen.

"I'm taking her to the park today. What are you doing? Are you going to stay in the city? At least you're not too far away this time. You can pop in for a visit."

"With this third murder, I'll be here for at least another week, but it looks like I need to go back to Portland for some further investigation."

Her mother ran a hand through her still-lustrous dark hair streaked with silver. "I wish you'd take some nice desk job and settle down. Kendall needs a father and some stability."

Christina put a hand over her heart where the guilt stabbed her. "Kendall has a father and right now you're providing the stability, Mom. After this case, I'm planning on doing more profile work. Believe me, I'll be spending lots of time at my desk."

"Yeah, well about Kendall's father…"

"Oops, gotta go, Ma. Have fun at the park and if you have time take Kendall for a shaved ice at that new place. She loves that stuff, even though half the ice ends up in her lap."

Her mom shook her head. "You need to get your life in order."

"I will. I am. Love you, Ma."

She ended the videoconferencing session and shoved the computer off her lap. She hated it when her mother was right.

She rolled off the bed and headed to the bathroom. Now that she had Charlie Fitch on her side, he'd invited her to the station today to review the report on the latest murder. The Portland P.D. had done some more background on the victim, and she had nothing in common with the previous victim in San Francisco or the woman yesterday— nothing except the tarot cards shoved between their cold, dead fingers.

And the other tarot card? Had there been another tarot card in the vicinity of the other victims that they'd missed?

She'd called her bureau chief, Rich Greavy, to report this recent finding, but she had to leave a message for him. The fact that he wouldn't take her call didn't surprise her. Even if he didn't get back to her, she knew he'd give his approval for her to return to the other crime scene in Portland—as long as she stayed out of his hair.

She showered and changed into yet another pantsuit, the unofficial uniform of the female FBI agent. She paired the beige slacks and jacket with a peach blouse and some sky-high heels. They went well with the .45 she'd strapped to her body.

Fifteen minutes later, she wheeled her small rental car

into the parking lot of the station. She strode through the squad room toward the detectives' area and knocked on the lieutenant's door.

"C'mon in."

She poked her head into his office. "Good morning, Charlie. Do you have the reports?"

"All ready to go." He tapped some file folders on his desk. "So the Bureau's sending one of your brethren out here to help you."

"Really?" She sealed her lips and fought the warmth that crept into her cheeks. Too late.

Fitch raised his brows. "You didn't know?"

No, because the Western Bureau Chief didn't believe female agents were competent to handle murder cases on their own.

"Ah, never got the confirmation." She shifted her purse from one shoulder to the other. "He's coming today?"

He picked up the thick file folders and waved them in the air. "Yep. Told him you'd be here this morning and I'd have the reports ready for the two of you."

"Yeah, great. Looks like we'll be putting together a task force on this case, or at least a task force of two."

"Swell." He dropped the file folders on his blotter.

And just like that, Greavy had probably wrecked the tentative rapport she'd established with Fitch.

Leaning over his desk, she scooped up the reports. "If you have someplace for me to sit, I'll get out of your way and wait for the other agent."

"To your right, three doors down there's an empty office. You're welcome to use it until your partner in crime fighting shows up."

"Thanks, Charlie. Coffee?"

"No, thanks."

Pursing her lips, she glared at the bald spot on his head as he bent over his desk. "I meant for me."

Without an ounce of embarrassment, he aimed a stubby finger toward the door. "Back in the squad room."

"Thanks a lot." She clicked his door shut and blew out a breath. Yep, that rapport was totally trashed.

Her high heels clicked on the linoleum as she hugged the file folders to her chest and made her way back to the squad room.

Christina balanced the file folders on the edge of the counter and shook a disposable cup loose from a stack.

"Do you want me to get that for you?"

Christina glanced over her shoulder at a fresh-faced female cop, her hair pulled back in a tight ponytail. "I think I got it."

The officer reached around Christina for the coffeepot. "That's okay. You'd better grab those folders instead."

Snatching the case files from the counter, Christina laughed. "You're right. Those almost landed on the floor."

"Not that I wouldn't mind getting a look at them." The woman aimed a steady stream of steaming brown liquid into Christina's cup.

"Is that so, Officer…" She squinted at the cop's name tag. "Griego?"

"Yes, ma'am." She replaced the coffeepot on the hot plate. "I've been on patrol for two years now, and I'm just itching to take the detective's exam."

"Homicide?"

"That's my goal."

Christina raised her cup to Officer Griego. "If I need some help, I'll make a request for you."

"Thank you, ma'am. I'd appreciate that."

As Officer Griego turned away, Christina grimaced and tipped some cream into her cup. *You hit thirty and you become ma'am.*

She blew on the surface of her coffee as she made her way back to the office Fitch had indicated before. She dropped the file folders on the desk, leaving the door open behind her. The open-door policy seemed to work better with the police departments, and she just might need Officer Griego's help.

She flipped open the covers of the two files and reached for a third tucked into her briefcase. She positioned the case file for the Portland murder next to the other two. The tarot cards and the M.O. tied two murders in San Francisco to the one in Portland. No doubt about it.

Why only one in Portland and two here? Had they missed a second one in Portland? If these were random, then the killer must've been in Portland for business or pleasure. Or maybe he lived in Oregon and San Francisco was the trip away from home, but the Oregon murder had come between the two in the city.

The close succession of the two murders here had allowed her to see the crime scene for herself this time. When the tarot card had been discovered on the body of the murder victim in Portland, just like it had here, the Bureau had sent her back to San Francisco to follow up.

Then the killer struck again while she was in the city. Lucky for her—not so much for the victim.

For the next hour, she buried her nose in the papers in between sips of lukewarm coffee. Nobody had disturbed her until Officer Griego tapped on the office door.

"Ma'am?"

Christina looked up and rubbed one eye. "Yes?"

"The other agent from the Bureau is here." Griego looked ready to burst with pride as if she'd personally invited him here and tracked her down.

"Thanks. Send him on over."

Officer Griego's rosy cheeks got rosier. "He's right…"

A tall, broad form filled the door behind the tiny officer. "Thanks, Rita. I'll take it from here."

Christina clenched her jaw to keep it from hitting the desk. Then she eked out a tight smile and said hello to Eric Brody, her ex-fiancé, the love of her life and the father of her child.

Chapter Two

Christina looked ready to spit nails. Still didn't detract one bit from her all-around gorgeousness.

He had the advantage knowing about this meeting beforehand, and if there's one thing he'd learned about his ex-fiancée it was that if you had an advantage over her—exploit it.

She reined herself in and the tight lips curved into a tighter smile. "You're back."

"In the flesh." He spread his arms, spanning the doorway.

Two spots of color flagged her cheeks and then disappeared almost immediately. She recovered quickly—always had, always would.

"I heard you were traipsing around Latin America after your…leave of absence." Her fingers drummed the papers on the desk.

He kicked the door shut behind him and she jumped. Not so composed after all.

"I've been back in the States about a month. Went straight from drugs to serial killers."

"Are you okay with the move?" Her dark, liquid eyes softened as they scanned his face, and her long lashes fluttered against her cheeks.

The edges of his cold resolve melted just a little. Then

he straightened his spine. He'd seen that look before—right before she stabbed him in the back.

"Why not?" He lifted his shoulders in a quick shrug. "I'm particularly suited to the assignment, don't you agree? Just like I was particularly suited to the kidnapping detail. Let's just hope this one ends better."

She jumped from her chair, smacking her palms on the desk blotter. "You…"

He held up his hands.

She closed her eyes, adjusted the waistband of her slacks and plopped back in her chair. "You look good."

His gaze strayed from the perfect oval of her face to her long fingers twisting into knots. He could say the same for her. The masculine pantsuit did nothing to conceal her femininity, and from the way she towered over the desk he knew her feet were slipped into those high heels she loved to wear at the office to remind everyone in this male-dominated field that she was still a woman.

Not that there could be any doubt about that. Ever.

"You look good, too. Serial killers agree with you. Of course, they always did. You must be in heaven."

A spasm crumpled her face and she shoved the file folders toward him. "Oh, yeah. It's heaven to see young women like Nora and Olivia cut down in the prime of life by some sick whack job."

Heaving out a long sigh, he rolled a leather-bound chair behind him and dropped into it. The war between them was over. He'd ended the engagement, and these battles were unnecessary. "I'm sorry, Christina. That was a low blow. The families of these women are lucky to have you on their cases."

Her lips parted and she nodded. Her mouth had lost the tightness and looked totally kissable—and God he could take her in his arms right now and do justice to those luscious lips.

The lust that slammed him and had him shifting in the squeaky chair hadn't revved him up like this in over two years—the last time he'd seen Christina Sandoval.

Greavy was a sadistic SOB to put him on this case with Christina. Of course, Greavy had no idea the homicide in San Diego he'd assigned to Eric as soon as he joined the unit would be linked to Christina's three cases in Portland and San Francisco. This guy got around.

Clearing his throat, he folded his arms behind his head and tipped back in his chair, making it squeak even more. "Did Rich tell you why I was coming out?"

"Rich didn't tell me you were coming out at all."

"I mean, did he tell you why another agent was joining you?"

"Typical Greavy. I haven't spoken to him in person since he sent me to Portland. I had to find out another agent was coming to assist me from Lieutenant Fitch over there." She spun the file folders around to face him. "And here you are."

He cocked his head. "Greavy didn't tell you about the other case in San Diego?"

"There was another murder in San Diego? Same M.O.?"

"Yep."

A flare of anger turned her cheeks red. "I'm assuming the killer stuck the tarot card with the maiden and lion between the vic's fingers. Three murders up here, three tarot cards."

"This is where it gets weird. The body had a tarot card between his fingers, all right, but it wasn't that lion one."

Christina's eyes widened. "Let me guess. It was a tarot card with a fool on it."

Eric leaned forward and the front wheels of his chair hit the floor where it skidded a few inches to the right. "How'd you know that?"

"I canvased the area where we found the most recent victim, Nora Sterling. I thought I had a pretty good idea where the killer was hiding before he attacked her—up a tree. I climbed the tree and found the card."

"What made you climb the tree?" But he didn't have to ask. Christina always claimed she could get into the head of a killer. He still didn't know if he believed her or not, but it could come in handy in this case if she could.

"Just…umm, a feeling and some damage to the bark on the trunk."

"Do you have the card here?" He shuffled through the papers in the case folders.

"It's in evidence."

"Prints?"

"None."

Eric whistled through his teeth. "I wonder if there were any more tarot cards near the body in San Diego."

"I was wondering the same thing about the murder in Portland and the first one here." She tapped a pencil against her chin and then dropped it. "Wait. Did you say the victim in San Diego was male?"

"That's right."

"Was the body found outdoors? Bludgeoned and then throat slit?"

"Nope—indoors, no bludgeoning, but his throat was slit. He lost an amazing amount of blood that soaked into the carpet and the floorboards beneath."

"Same with the other victims. They suffered a lot of blood loss." She curled her fingers around the arms of the chair. "So the M.O. was a little different for the male victim."

"We did find some drugs and alcohol in his system, so maybe the killer incapacitated him that way and didn't have to hit him over the head."

"That suggests he knew him or had some kind of contact with him before the murder. That doesn't seem to be the case at all with the women."

Christina sucked in her bottom lip, which she always did when she was thinking. She couldn't just be trying to focus his attention on her mouth, could she? Because he couldn't keep his eyes, or his nasty thoughts, off her lips.

"What could possibly be the connection between these four people?"

Clearing his throat, he scratched the stubble on his chin. "I guess it's up to us to find the connections, because they have to be there."

"Us. There hasn't been an us for a long time."

"I think we can be adults and work together." As soon as he could get his mind out of the gutter.

"Sure." She folded her hands on the desk. "How's your family?"

"Fine. Yours? How's your mother?"

"She's doing well, busy."

"Busy? I thought she retired from nursing."

Christina's hands got fidgety again, stacking papers and lining up pencils. She'd never been the nervous type before. She'd always had a cool, calm demeanor. As cold as ice—except in the bedroom.

Seeing him had rattled her.

His response to her had surprised him, too. He accepted the fact that he'd never forget Christina, no matter what she'd done to him, but he'd believed he could tame the visceral reaction she'd always elicited from him. Not so much.

He dragged his gaze away from her puckered lips as she blew a strand of dark hair from her face.

"She did retire, but she picked up a bunch of hobbies."

"Good for her." He pointed at the folders. "How about it? Do you want to get a couple of sandwiches delivered and dig in to what we got?"

"Sounds good. I'll ask our new best friend, Officer Griego, for some suggestions."

"Yeah, there's some hero worship going on there."

"You always did have the ladies fawning over you."

He raised one eyebrow. "I was talking about you. From the minute she volunteered to take me to you, it was Agent Sandoval this, Agent Sandoval that."

Christina gave an unladylike snort. "Did you set her straight?"

"I didn't have time."

Her nostrils flared as she reached for the phone and punched the speaker button and three other buttons. "Hi, Officer Griego. Can you recommend a good take-out place in the area for lunch?"

"One of the sergeants is taking orders now for the deli down the street. I'll send him over."

"That would be great. Menu?"

"I'll bring one to you."

Christina rolled her eyes at him. "That's not necessary. We'll come out and have a look."

"That's okay, ma'am. I know you and Agent Brody are busy. I'll bring the menu right in. Sarge won't mind."

"Thanks, Officer Griego." She pressed the speaker button and ended the call.

Eric twisted his lips into a smile. "I'm sure Sarge *will* mind catering to the two fibbies in his midst."

"They seem okay with me here, so far. Have you met Lieutenant Fitch yet? I had him eating out of my hand yesterday, but he turned cold once he knew you were on the way."

"I don't get these guys. They should be happy for the help. My brother Ryan always is."

"Is he still working up the coast in Crestview?"

"Yep."

Officer Griego peered through the window waving the menu and knocked on the door.

Eric scooted his chair back and opened the door. "C'mon in."

She thrust the menu at him. "It's pretty basic."

"That's what we like—basic." He tossed the menu to Christina.

Wrinkling her nose, she ran the tip of her finger down the glossy page. "I'll take the California on sourdough, but…"

"No mayo and extra pickles." Eric finished for her.

She tilted her head, her shiny, dark ponytail slipping over her shoulder. "That predictable, huh?"

Warmth spread through his chest. He hadn't meant to finish her sentence, didn't want her to know how much he remembered.

"Well, you always were kind of picky."

Rita was standing at the door hanging on their every word, wide-eyed.

Eric glanced at the menu and handed it back to her saying, "The Italian, fries and a drink—something with caffeine."

"I'll give your order to Sergeant Hammond. It usually takes about forty-five minutes."

Eric reached into his pocket for some cash and handed her two twenties. "Thanks, Rita and thank the sarge for us, too."

"You're welcome. Anything else I can do for you?"

Christina gave her one of her sweet smiles that seemed to have gotten even sweeter. "We're good. Thanks so much for your help."

Rita practically bowed out of the room, closing the door behind her.

Eric jerked his thumb at the door. "What do you think she expects out of all this? It's not like you can give her a recommendation for homicide."

"Maybe she thinks you can pull some strings with your brother."

"Sean? Rita's in the same department. She should know

by now Detective Sean Brody is not a quid pro quo kinda guy. He expects everyone to work hard to get ahead." He leveled a finger at Christina. "Besides, it's you she idolizes."

"I think she just wants to learn. The men in the department probably aren't very encouraging and maybe she doesn't have any role models here."

"You didn't need any role models."

"I was a special case. Didn't you always tell me that?"

Drawing his chair toward the desk, he hunched forward. "What drove you up that tree, Christina?"

"I told you—a hunch."

"One of *those* hunches? Did you feel anything?"

She squeezed her eyes closed and massaged her left temple. "Incredible evil."

"Did you tell the P.D. here?"

She gave a short laugh, almost a bark. "Are you kidding? I want to be taken seriously, not written off as a crackpot."

"The Bureau has used psychics before."

"I'd hardly call myself a psychic, and honestly, the Bureau may use them but most don't respect them. Greavy sure doesn't."

"Like I told you before, it's a talent you should try to develop."

She hugged herself. "I don't know if I want to develop it. Besides, in this case, I didn't get much at all, just a feeling."

"Up to you." Eric checked his watch. "Let's get started before lunch gets here."

"Umm, do you want to wheel around here? I'll take you through the first San Francisco murder."

He walked his chair to her side of the desk and at once her scent overwhelmed him. The familiar musky perfume wrapped its tendrils around him, but the essence of Christina had a stronger impact on him.

He couldn't put his finger on it. He never could and it had haunted him ever since the day he cut her loose.

She dragged a file folder between them on the desk and flipped it open. She spread a stack of photos in front of him, and green, leafy, verdant forest blurred together.

"Was it another running trail?"

"Hiking, just across the bay."

He thumbed through the photos. "Victim?"

"Liz Fielding, late forties, single. Some trouble in her past but clean for at least five years."

"What kind of trouble?"

"Some drugs, petty theft, a little hooking."

"What about the other two?"

"Haven't dug up anything like that yet, but the investigation is still young."

He plucked out the pictures of the body. She'd been positioned like his male victim in San Diego—stretched out on her back, hands positioned over her stomach, the tarot slipped between her fingers. He traced a finger over her disheveled clothes.

"No sexual assault, huh?"

"Nope, not for any of the victims. Your guy?"

"No." He shook out another photo, this one a close-up of the victim's throat and the ghastly, gaping wound. A necklace clung to the woman's neck, still intact.

Eric's pulse jumped and he held the picture closer to his face.

"What is it? You see something?"

He dropped the photo and he jabbed a finger at the victim's throat. "This necklace…same one my kidnapper wore."

Chapter Three

Christina jerked her head to the side, her jaw dropping. Was Eric seeing things? He'd rarely mentioned his kidnapping as an eleven-year-old in San Francisco. It had been a strange one—no ransom note, no demands, and the kidnappers released him on a street corner two days later.

At the time, the police had connected his kidnapping to the serial killer case Eric's father had been working— the serial killings Joseph Brody would later be suspected of committing. Right before he jumped from the Golden Gate Bridge.

What did this murder victim, Liz Fielding, have to do with Eric's kidnapping?

She snatched up the photo from the desk where he'd dropped it. "What are you talking about, Eric? Her necklace?"

"She kept her face hidden, they all did. I guess they figured that was easier than blindfolding me. And the woman, she's the one who always checked on me. When she leaned over me, her necklace would swing forward. I got a good look at the medallion hanging from the chain." He tapped the picture. "Just like this."

She squinted at the necklace with the round pendant nestled against the dead woman's chest. "It's just a coincidence, Eric."

He closed his eyes and pinched the bridge of his nose. "I always thought it was some symbol of Satan or something."

"And why wouldn't you?" She studied the design of the symbol, black etching on the silver disc. It almost looked like the outline of a whale's tail, but she could see how a child might see a pair of horns.

"Did you ever research it?"

"Honestly, I'd forgotten all about the design until two minutes ago."

"How can you even be sure it's the same symbol after all these years?"

"You have your feelings, and I—" he poked his chest with his thumb "—have mine."

"It's not the same necklace, Eric. This is not the same woman."

"The age is right. My kidnapper was probably mid-twenties. This woman is mid-forties."

"Eric." She gripped his wrist. "Liz Fielding is not the same woman who kidnapped you. She's wearing a similar necklace."

Licking his lips, he wiped the back of his hand across his forehead. "You're right. It just took me back. Crazy."

He opened the desk drawer and slipped out a piece of paper. He started sketching on it with his pencil.

"Now what?"

"I didn't have access to a computer or the internet twenty years ago. Now I'm curious what, if anything, this symbol means. Who knows? The meaning of Liz's necklace might even lead to a break in this case." He lodged his tongue in the corner of his mouth and continued drawing.

While Eric took his walk down memory lane, she perused the crime scene photos, checking them against the report. The detectives in Portland hadn't identified a location where the killer could've been lying in wait, but he must've done so. He'd had his killing accoutrement with him, a blunt object for stunning his victim, a sharp knife for the cutting and the tarot card for the coup de grâce.

Maybe it wasn't going to be Liz Fielding that day, but it was going to be someone.

She'd have to make a return visit to the area where Liz had been found and take Eric with her. She slid a glance at his face, the lines set in concentration.

He still made her pulse race, and warm, sweet honey pool in all the right places.

He'd broken her heart when he walked out on her. By the time she'd discovered her pregnancy he'd gone on a leave of absence and escaped to parts unknown.

Even when she'd heard he was back on the job, she couldn't bring herself to contact him and tell him about Kendall. He probably would've accused her of using Kendall to get him back.

Once he'd discovered her notes about the Phone Book Killer, it had completely destroyed any trust between them. She'd been so outraged that he believed Ray's lies about her, she didn't bother explaining the truth to him. When she found out she was pregnant, it was too late. He'd disappeared from her life…but apparently not for good.

"There." He ended the drawing with a flourish. "I'm going to track this down."

"I hope it does mean something."

Someone tapped on the door and they scooted their chairs apart as if they'd been cheating on an exam.

Officer Griego waved through the window and held up a white bag.

"Come in, Rita."

She pushed into the room carrying the bag in one hand and a drink in the other. "Here you go. The other drink's on the table outside."

Eric jumped from his chair and took the bag and soda from her and put them on the desk. "Thanks."

She handed him the other drink and a fistful of money. "Here's your change."

"That's okay." He waved a hand. "Put it in the lunch kitty."

"Will do. Enjoy your lunch. Let me know if you need anything."

Eric tapped his black bag on the floor with the toe of his shoe. "Wi-Fi for my laptop?"

"Absolutely."

"Thanks, Rita."

Christina peeked into the bag that already had a spot of grease forming on it. "I hope they got my sandwich right."

"Hand it over, Sandoval. I'm starving."

She dug his sandwich and a cone of fries from the bag and held them up. "Where do you want them?"

He took the bag from her, pulled her sandwich out and then ripped the bag open and spread it out on the desk. "Right here."

She placed his food on the bag and snatched a French fry. "Now I know where all that grease came from."

"Greasy fries, just the way I like them. Nothing beats those fish and chips at Scolino's on the Wharf, though."

She bit into her sandwich and nodded while Eric reached into his bag on the floor and pulled out his laptop.

"I'm going to fire this up and do what I couldn't twenty years ago."

"What? Online dating?" She chuckled at her own joke and peeked under her bread to make sure the extra pickles were in place.

"Why? Have you given it a try?" He tapped the power button on his laptop and then reached across it to grab his sandwich.

She almost choked on a pickle. She hadn't even given old-fashioned dating a try since having Kendall, let alone the online kind. "No. Have you?"

She swallowed and held her breath.

"I don't think the Bureau would look too kindly on one of its agents trolling online dating sites while working in a foreign country."

He hadn't tried it because of his job, not because he didn't want to. She sipped her soda to avoid blurting the first jealous thing out of her mouth. She had no right to be jealous or to care who or how he was dating.

Their engagement was over. He'd ended it when he found her notes on his father's case and chose to believe Ray Lopez, a reporter, over her about what she planned to do with them. But she had to be honest with herself. That discovery may have spurred him on, that and the disastrous ending to the kidnapping case he'd been working, but they'd been having fundamental differences about where to take their relationship.

Kids—that had been the fundamental difference. And now they had one and he didn't know a thing about her.

"Where should I start looking?" Eric flattened his drawing on the desk next to the computer. "Symbols? Signs? Demonic symbols?"

"Try all three." She pilfered another French fry from his pile and then dusted the salt off her fingertips.

He held a hand over his food. "If you wanted fries, why didn't you order them?"

"Because there are so many more calories in a full order that you can eat all by yourself than a few stolen fries." She hunched forward as he scrolled down the page containing websites about satanic symbols.

"Right. When did you ever worry about counting calories?" His gaze darted to his right and then returned and wandered down her body. "Although…"

Prickles of heat danced across her flesh in the wake of his inventory as her body called out for his in every way.

She grabbed another fry and waved it in his face to

distract him from the subtle responses shifting through every cell of her being. "Are you trying to say I've gained weight?"

He blinked and turned back to the screen. "A little, but it suits you."

"Just great." She patted her stomach. "That's exactly what you want to hear from someone after two years apart."

He snorted and tapped the keyboard. "Don't pretend to be the insulted party, Christina. You were skinny before and now you're not so skinny. You've filled out in all the right places and you look great. There—I said it. You can stop fishing for compliments now."

With her eyes stinging, she took a big bite of her sandwich. He still saw her as devious and conniving, even over something petty like her appearance. How could she ever tell him about Kendall when he still harbored such resentment against her?

She watched his strong hands as they hovered over the keyboard. Resentful he may be, but he hadn't gotten her out of his blood any more than she'd gotten him out of hers. His brain might be telling him no, but his male libido was sending an entirely different message—one that she read loud and clear.

She'd been on only a handful of dates in the past few years, but she recognized the look of lust in a man's eyes when she saw it—especially in Eric's eyes. She'd seen it there enough times when the passion between them ran hot and undeniable.

"Who knew there were so many satanic symbols?"

She cleared her throat. "Maybe it's not satanic. Maybe it has something to do with Mother Nature or Buddhism or something."

"I'm looking at all three women now and I don't see much of a connection between them. Olivia Dearing was a waitress in Portland. Liz Fielding worked as a nurse's aide, and Nora worked in a bookstore."

Eric tapped a pencil against his stubbled chin. "They're all service jobs. Maybe they ran into someone in the course of their day who tagged them for murder."

"Maybe, although the women don't look much alike, so if it's a random selection of victims it's harder to connect the dots."

"At least we know he traveled from Portland to San Francisco to San Diego and back to San Francisco at some point, which leads me to believe he lives here."

She lined up pictures of the three women in life side by side, and pointed to each one. "He travels for work, he eats out, he visits someone in the hospital."

"Liz didn't work in a hospital. She did home health care." He nudged aside the finger she had planted on Liz Fielding's picture with his own.

She snatched her hand away from his warm touch and dropped it in her lap. Then she closed her eyes and took a deep breath. If she wanted to give him the impression that his hard body and smoldering eyes had absolutely no effect on her, she'd better up her game.

"Are you okay?"

Her eyes flew open and she met his concerned gaze. Concern? She'd figured that emotion would be in short supply from him. They were making progress.

"You're not getting any of those feelings, are you?"

"From a few photos?" She coughed and plucked a tissue from the box on the credenza behind her. "Not likely."

"The cards?"

"Didn't have enough time." She snapped her fingers. "We're forgetting all about your San Diego victim."

"I haven't forgotten about him." He reached into his bag, pulled out a bulging accordion file and hoisted it onto his lap.

"I mean, what did he do for a living?"

"Shoes."

"Shoe salesman?" She scooted to the edge of her seat. "Another job with customer contact."

"Women's shoes."

She dug her elbows into the desk blotter and rested her chin in one palm. "It doesn't mean our killer didn't notice him there. Department store shoes?"

"A shoe store in a mall."

"Better yet. The Tarot Card Killer saw him eating lunch at the food court."

Eric raised his eyebrows. "The Tarot Card Killer? You've given him a moniker already?"

"He gave it to himself. Not—" she created a cross with her two index fingers "—in that way. I just mean it's kind of an obvious name for him, isn't it?"

"I guess thinking of a catchy name for a serial killer isn't something I do right out of the box on an investigation." He slid the band off the file with a snap. "I leave that to the reporters."

Heat scorched her cheeks. Did she just think they were making progress? Scratch that.

"Excuse me, Mr. Get-Down-to-Business." She swept her trash from lunch into the wastepaper basket and reached for the papers spilling from his accordion file. "Now let's get down to business."

They managed to work side by side for the next four hours without either one of them throwing a punch…or stealing a kiss.

Christina pushed back her chair and stretched, interlacing her fingers over her head. "I'm done."

"I think we have a good start here. I'm willing to turn over our notes to the SFPD if you are."

"Sure. Maybe something we pulled out will resonate with them."

"I know they went to the bookstore where Nora worked, but I'd like to have a look myself. The Kindred Spirit doesn't sound like your run-of-the-mill bookstore."

"It's an independent. That name could mean anything."

"Yeah, but whatever it is, Detective Winston didn't make note of it here." He thumbed through the papers from the P.D.'s case file.

Christina gathered her three folders together and shoved them into her briefcase yawning open on the floor beside her. "Where are you staying?"

"Same place as you."

"Great." Her lips stretched into a polite, professional smile. *Damn.* Someone up there wanted to torture her. "You can follow me over in your car. It's not far."

"Well, I would if I had a car."

She pinched her finger with the latch of her briefcase and then sucked it into her mouth. Someone *really* wanted to torture her.

"I took a taxi from the airport, left my suitcase in the squad room. I'll just hitch a ride with you."

"Sounds…good." She wheeled back her chair and grabbed her purse from the credenza. She plucked her cell phone from the side pocket and checked the display, cupping her hand around it. She'd have to swap out the wallpaper photo of Kendall unless she wanted Eric to start asking uncomfortable questions.

The guilt washed over her in such a strong wave, her knees wobbled and she plopped back into the chair. She glanced quickly at Eric, but he was busy packing up his own stuff and didn't notice her sudden collapse.

How could she keep Eric in the dark any longer? All the reasons she'd used to put off telling him about her pregnancy, including the fact that she didn't know where he'd gone on his leave of absence, came tumbling down around her. She had no excuses left.

He probably still didn't want kids and his last kidnapping case with the Bureau had pretty much reinforced that for him, but he should still know about his daughter's existence.

And Kendall? She deserved to know her father even if he didn't remain a constant fixture in her life—not that an absentee father ever did *her* any good.

As a child she'd even wished her father had already died some noble death instead of constantly confronting the hurt and pain that he just didn't want her in his life if she wasn't going to conform to his lifestyle.

But Eric was nothing like her father.

"Why are you still sitting there? You ready to go?"

"Just waiting for you." She gripped the handle of her briefcase and slung her purse over her shoulder. She scooted from behind the desk, waving Eric through the door first.

She didn't need to squeeze past him, brushing body parts, feeling the warmth of his flesh. It was bad enough they'd be sharing a car and a hotel.

They shuffled into the squad room to a few nods and a big smile from Officer Griego.

"Any breaks in the case?"

"Not yet. Have a good night." Eric retrieved his suitcase from the corner and they stopped by the lieutenant's office on their way out. His blinds were drawn and they could hear voices from inside.

Eric sliced a finger across his throat and pointed to the exit.

"Are you in the parking garage?"

"Too crowded. I'm in the lot across the street."

They emerged into the sunlight and Christina took a deep breath of fresh air as she fished for her sunglasses in her purse. "You don't realize you've been cooped up all day until you get outside."

"It's always a good idea to take a breather." Eric slipped

his own sunglasses out of his front pocket. "Now we just have a few hours left of daylight."

"I'm over here." She held her arm out and clicked the remote. "Do you even plan to get your own rental car?"

"With all the budget cuts in place? I'm lucky I got my own room in the hotel."

She sent him a sidelong glance but sealed her lips. She wouldn't go there. "At least the hotel is halfway decent."

They approached the rental from the rear, and Christina popped the trunk.

Eric stepped beside her, nudging her shoulder with his and took the briefcase from her hand.

"Here, I'll get that."

"Thanks." Would she ever get to the point where she could stand next to this man without going all gooey inside? She skirted the bumper and headed to the front of the car.

"What the heck is this on my windshield?"

Eric slammed the trunk and the little car bounced. "Parking ticket? I'm sure Rita Griego would be more than happy to take care of that for you."

"It's not paper." She bent forward to get a closer look at the white mark in the corner of her windshield. Her belly flip-flopped.

Eric circled around the front of the car to the driver's side. "What is it?"

She straightened up and turned to face him. "It's our sign. It's the sign from Liz Fielding's necklace."

Chapter Four

Eric's jaw tightened and he ducked around Christina to get a better look. The symbol mocked him, and he felt like smashing his fist through the glass.

Why had he never remembered the necklace and that symbol before now? He may have told the police about it after the kidnapping, had probably even described it to them, but he must've erased it from his memory after that.

Christina stiffened beside him and grabbed his arm. "Who put it there?"

Turning, he scanned the parking lot, his gaze traveling across the lampposts. "There aren't any cameras here, so we're out of luck."

"It must be someone connected to Liz's murder." Her fingernails clawed at his flesh through his suit jacket.

"Or maybe just someone connected to Liz." He smacked the roof of the car. "We need to find out what that symbol means, and we're going to start by going to Nora's bookstore."

"Nora's bookstore?" She snapped a couple of pictures of the symbol with her phone's camera.

"The Kindred Spirit. Think about it. Sounds like one of those fantasy, sci-fi places." He leaned forward and scraped the edge of the white markings with his thumbnail. "White shoe polish."

"Do you want to head over there right now?"

"It can wait. I need to get out of this suit. I'll make sure the store is open later." He pulled out his phone and slid into the car. He tapped in a search for the bookstore and checked the location and hours. "They're open until midnight—the witching hour."

"Technically, midnight is not the witching hour. That would be 3:00 a.m., sort of the opposite of the time Christ was born at 3:00 p.m."

"And you would know."

"Did you just call me a witch?"

He glanced at Christina's profile. Her smile was bright but brittle. He'd have to tread lightly. Too much unfinished business and animosity lay between them. "Isn't your half sister into some of this stuff?"

She loosened her grip on the steering wheel. "Yep. She inherited some of my father's particular gifts just like I did, and she ran with them."

"How close are you to her? Maybe she could help us with this sign."

"Not that close. I haven't spoken to her in over a month, and I'm not comfortable discussing these things with her."

"Okay. Forget that."

She wheeled the car into the circular driveway of the hotel. "Do you want me to drop you off in the front?"

"Just park. I can wheel my suitcase in."

She made the turn and slid a card into the slot for the parking arm, which creaked open. "Do you think I'm being followed?"

"Someone knows you're working this case and knows your car."

"Do you think that sign on the windshield is there to tell me something or threaten me?"

"I don't know, Christina. Either way, it's a break."

"Either way, we need to inform Rich."

He hauled his suitcase from the trunk and piled Christina's briefcase and his own bag on top of it. She waited while he approached the front desk.

"Checking in. Brody."

"I have your reservation right here, Mr. Brody, room 632."

Christina made a sharp movement beside him. "I'm in 634."

The clerk tapped a few keys on her keyboard. "Those two rooms are connected. That was a special request on the reservation for Mr. Brody."

Eric held up one hand. "It wasn't me. Travel made my arrangements."

The hotel clerk's gaze darted from him to Christine. "D-do you want a different room?"

"It's fine."

"Fine." Christina echoed in a faint voice.

Eric tapped his Bureau credit card on the counter once before handing it to the clerk. He had to get ahold of his professionalism here. But why had the Bureau decided it was a good idea to pair him with his ex-fiancée on a case? Of course, it wasn't the Bureau who had made that decision. It was the killer when he decided to leave those tarot cards on his vic in San Diego, linking that crime with Christina's three cases.

He followed Christina's clicking heels, dragging his suitcase behind him, trying to keep his eyes off her swaying hips.

She'd always been slim and athletic with some nice curves. Now those curves had become dangerous. She'd filled out where it mattered most.

Professional, Brody.

They got off the elevator and Christina stopped halfway down the hallway. "That's yours and this is mine."

"I'll try to keep the noise down."

She slid her key card into her door. "Well, let me know when you're ready to head out to Kindred Spirits."

"Do you want to join me for dinner first?" He'd suggest that to any colleague, wouldn't he?

Her long lashes fluttered. "Sure. Knock on my door when you're ready."

Eric stepped into the room, closed the door and slumped against it, allowing the facade to slip from his body. He'd always been able to be himself around Christina, but now he felt as if he had to hold himself in check.

He shrugged out of his suit jacket and hung it in the closet. He crossed the room to the window and paused half-way there, glancing at the door that connected his room to Christina's.

He didn't need the temptation, but if he requested a different room he'd come off looking weak or worse, as if he really cared that she was on the other side of the wall sleeping, undressing, showering.

He smacked his fist into his palm. He could get through this assignment.

Filmy, white drapes covered the windows and he yanked them back to reveal a view of Union Square. He'd grown up in this city. Knew it like the lines crisscrossing his palms, but his job with the FBI had taken him all over the place, including D.C. where he lived now. Could he ever live here again with the constant reminders of his family tragedy, and views of the Golden Gate Bridge from vantage points all over the city?

He left the drapes open and crashed across the bed. It was high time he came to terms with that past, including his kidnapping as a child.

He stared at the ceiling for several seconds until he heard the shower from Christina's room. He toed off his shoes and sat up on the edge of the bed where he got rid of his socks and loosened his tie.

Dinner and then the bookstore—no drinks, no casual conversation, no flirting. Definitely no flirting.

He shed the rest of his clothing and padded into the tiled bathroom. Bracing his hands on the vanity, he hunched closer to the mirror. What did she see when she looked at him? Had he changed in the past two years like she had?

Because she *had* changed. He couldn't put his finger on it. She seemed softer, less brittle. Maybe in stoking his anger against her, he'd built up her hard shell in his mind.

He'd watched for it, but he never did see that book come out about his father. Never saw any wedding announcement for Christina and Ray Lopez either. Not that he still didn't see Lopez around.

In fact, Lopez had been sniffing around his brother's case recently, trying to poke at old wounds. Sean had shown Lopez a lot more courtesy than he would have. Of course, Lopez had never been in cahoots with Sean's fiancée either.

Eric stepped into the shower and let a steady stream of hot water cascade down his back. He rolled his shoulders to get the kinks out. The leave of absence had done him good. He didn't want to have to take another after this case.

He twisted the towel around his waist. His toes sank into the carpet as he approached his suitcase in the corner where he'd parked it, his garment bag folded across the top. He hung up the garment bag in the closet and unzipped the suitcase.

He pawed through some shirts on the top and pulled out a pair of jeans. Dropping the jeans on the floor, he scooped up an armful of shirts and shook out each one before laying it out on the bed.

The knock on the adjoining door made him drop a shirt. "Yeah?"

"Are you ready for dinner yet?"

His gaze flicked to the towel slipping from his waist. "Give me a few more minutes."

"I'm starving."

"Five minutes."

He left the shirts on the bed, grabbed a clean pair of underwear and stepped into his jeans. A sharp knock on the door halted his progress back to the bathroom.

"Ready yet?"

Blowing out a breath, he crossed to the connecting door, unlocked it and yanked it open. "Impatient, aren't you?"

She made some reply that didn't register with his brain—because all reasoning had fled the scene, crowded out by his visceral emotions.

Christina had shed the pantsuit and replaced it with a pair of dark skinny jeans topped with a wide-necked red sweater that slid off one shoulder, revealing a black lacy tank top. Her loose, dark hair tumbled around her shoulders, and she tossed it back as she sized him up with narrowed eyes.

"You're not even dressed."

He dipped his chin to his bare chest. "Almost there. You had the advantage of being here a few days. I went straight to the P.D. from the airport."

"Excuses, excuses, Brody. Put some clothes on, will ya?"

He grunted and grabbed the shirt he'd dropped onto the bed. Had they slipped back into that easy camaraderie after just one afternoon spent together? That was part of Christina's charm. She came off like one of the guys, but lurking beneath the sarcastic banter was a potent sensuality that could lure you in and wrap you up before you even knew what hit you.

Now that he knew all her tricks, he could resist her. He stuffed his arms in the sleeves of his shirt and his nostrils flared. Her exotic perfume wafted across the room and slid into his shirt with him.

"Did you bring the case files with you?" As he buttoned

up the shirt in front of the mirror, his eyes strayed to her empty hands.

She arched an eyebrow. "I'm not bringing those to dinner. We know the basics. I have a notepad and pen in my purse just in case we have some amazing breakthrough."

He wouldn't bring case files to a normal working dinner either but this was no normal working dinner and he wanted the security of a distraction—a distraction from those dark, liquid eyes that shimmered with a hypnotic glow in candlelight.

"Give me one minute to make some sense of my hair." He retreated to the safety of the bathroom, but she followed him.

"Really? Eric Brody uses hair product now?" She curved against the doorjamb like a long, lean cat.

He rubbed the gel between his hands. "It's that or get a haircut."

"Don't do that. I like your hair longer." She tilted her head. "How do the big boys feel about the long hair?"

"They haven't said one way or the other, but then I don't see much of them." He rinsed his hands off in the sink and grabbed a towel.

"I'm sure they're just thrilled to get you back, long hair and all."

He stuffed the hand towel over the rack. "There are a couple of restaurants within walking distance to the hotel, but since we're going to hit the bookstore after dinner we might as well drive."

"There's a restaurant I've been wanting to try for a while. It's in the Haight-Ashbury district and should be pretty close to the bookstore, too."

"Sounds good." Anything sounded good about now—just to get out of this confined hotel room with Christina looking and smelling like sex on wheels.

Once in the parking garage, he stopped at the bumper of the little rental. "Do you want me to drive?"

"That's okay. The car's in my name." She clicked the remote. "We don't want to break any laws, especially with your brother, the SFPD detective, out on vacation."

He had no choice but to be a passenger in her car while she sat in the driver's seat. But he didn't have to be a passenger on this journey. He didn't have to be swept along a current of old feelings and desires. He'd been willing to give this woman everything, and she'd betrayed him…for a good story.

She swung the car into the line of traffic and sped up to avoid the cable car trundling to their right.

"It's a little tricky driving these streets."

"You're a native—you should be used to it by now."

"I didn't drive much when I lived here—walking and public transportation have always been the best ways to get around." She hunched over the steering wheel and peered at the road in front of her. "Do you think you'll ever move back to the city?"

"You know I'm in D.C. now? I like it but if opportunity knocked, I could make my home here again." He just might have to if he wanted to slay his demons.

"Do you plan to see your brothers while you're here?"

"As you already know, Sean's on an extended vacation, and I don't think Judd's in town either. I may take a trip up the coast to see Ryan."

"Yeah, Sean had an interesting case a few months ago."

"And Lopez was trying to get that story, too."

Christina bit her lower lip.

The silence in the car lasted just a few awkward minutes.

With her hand balanced on the top of the steering wheel, she pointed out the window. "I think we can park on this street for the restaurant and the bookshop."

She did an admirable parallel parking job, and he hopped

out of the car. The confines of the car ended up being a lot worse than the hotel. Dinner had to be better.

He opened the restaurant door for her and she brushed past him. Was she trying to drive him crazy?

The Friday night crowd was crammed into every table in the room and perched on every stool at the large circular bar in the middle of the restaurant.

"Ugh, I didn't even think about making a reservation."

Eric hunched toward the hostess stand. "How long is the wait?"

She ran the eraser end of her pencil down the columns of a book. "Just two?"

"Yes, and we promise we won't stay long."

"We just had a cancellation, so I can squeeze you in."

"Perfect." Eric slipped her a twenty as she turned to lead them to a table.

Christina pressed in next to him and whispered in his ear. "Must be that Brody charm."

As she pulled away, the strands of her hair tickled his neck.

Closing his eyes, he took a deep breath. He needed a good, stiff drink, and probably should stop thinking about a good, stiff anything.

The hostess led them to a decent table along the wall and tucked behind a plant.

"I don't know about you, but I need a drink."

Christina made a face. "I'm driving, so I'll abstain. Did you hear about Zollars?"

"DUI?"

"In a company car, on company business."

"Did he get his hand slapped?"

The waiter approached and Eric ordered a scotch, neat while Christina asked for ice water.

When the waiter left, Christina shook out her napkin

and draped it across her lap. "He got reprimanded and suspended for six weeks."

"Idiot."

"How was South America?"

"Hot and humid."

"I heard your team brought down a pretty high roller down there."

"We did all right. I heard you're making your mark on the serial killer unit. Dream come true, huh?"

She stopped fussing with her napkin and planted her elbows on the white tablecloth. "Can we just get this out of the way so you'll stop taking jabs at me?"

"Am I jabbing?" He knew damn well he was. It was the only thing keeping him from pulling her into his arms and kissing the smart aleck from her.

"You're too manly to play coy, Eric. I told you then, and I'm telling you now, I did not get into a relationship with you to get your father's story."

"But you wanted the Brody story."

"Joseph Brody's story has always fascinated me. I'm not gonna lie. But I had no intention of writing a book about your father."

"The notes?"

"Were notes. Something about your father's case always bothered me. I don't believe for one minute that he was the Phone Book Killer."

He pinched the bridge of his nose and when the waiter returned with his drink, he tossed back half of it. The smooth heat rolled down his throat and radiated throughout his chest.

"I've heard this before, Christina, but Ray Lopez told a different story."

She snorted. "If you had been in your right mind back then, you wouldn't have given Ray's story—any of Ray's story—a second thought."

She grabbed his hand, upsetting her waterglass. "I was your woman, Brody. I never would've betrayed you like that. The only reason you believed Ray over me was because of Noah Beckett. You were wrong about Noah, too."

The pain that sliced through his temples had him reaching for his glass. This time he downed the rest of the scotch and his eyes watered.

"I should've saved Noah."

"You followed the protocol for kidnappings. Noah would've met the same fate with anyone else at the helm."

"I was at the helm." He jabbed his chest with his thumb. "I should've known better. I was a kidnap victim myself. I should've done better by Noah. I should've done better by his parents."

"Just because you were a kidnap victim, didn't mean you had some magical power to save all other kidnap victims." Her nails dug into his forearm. "You did your job to the best of your ability, and the Becketts knew that."

"It wasn't good enough." He waved the waiter over. "Another scotch, please, and another napkin for the spilled water."

"Would you like to order now?" The waiter's eyes flicked back and forth between him and Christina.

"I'll have a Caesar salad and the steak, medium rare."

Christina ordered the salmon, and the waiter backed away from the table as if afraid to turn his back on them.

She pleated the napkin on the table. "If Noah's case hadn't come to its tragic end at the same time you found my notes, I know you would've given me a chance to explain, Eric."

He slumped against the banquette and rolled his glass between his palms. "Maybe you're right. The book never did come out, and you never married Lopez."

Her eyes popped open. "Marry Lopez? What gave you that crazy idea?"

"Lopez."

"And you believed him?" She grabbed the glass from his hand and took a gulp. Coughing, she slammed the glass back down on the table.

"It made sense at the time."

"At the time, you were in crazy town." She sniffed and dabbed a corner of the napkin under her bottom lashes.

She was right. He'd been out of his mind with grief and anger after losing Noah. When he'd turned to his fiancée for comfort and support, he'd found her notes about his father and his family and a nosy reporter feeding him lies.

Over the past few years, he'd had time to think about it all. It did seem pretty far-fetched that Christina would get into a relationship with him, agree to marry him, sleep with him—all to get the goods on his family tragedy to write a killer book.

She stuck out her hand, wiggling her fingers. "Can we call a truce while we're working on this case together?"

"Sure." He clasped her fingers, still chilly from mopping up the ice water. "I think I can even manage an apology. I overreacted to seeing those notes—bad timing all around."

She squeezed his hand. "Me, too. I should've never kept…that from you. I figured if I told you I had been researching your father's case, you'd think I was a creepy stalker."

"Truce." He dropped her hand and held up his own.

"So you're done with the well-aimed barbs?"

Truth was, he'd forgiven her a while back when he'd been on his leave of absence and was able to think clearly about the situation. It helped that no book had come out, and he hadn't heard anything linking her to Lopez.

And the barbs? Self-preservation against her charms. Just because he'd forgiven her didn't mean they should resume their engagement. She'd kept things from him, and he didn't like secrets—had grown up with too many of them.

"No barbs, well-aimed or otherwise." He pushed the rest of his drink aside and tore into a roll. The tension he'd been holding in his shoulders all day had slipped away. She'd been right about that, too—get everything out in the open.

They had a job to do.

Their food arrived and between bites, they discussed her cases and his task force in South America.

If someone had told him two years ago that he'd be sitting across the table from Christina laughing and sharing stories, he never would've believed it. The time off had done him good. Talking with his brothers had done him good.

As he signed the credit card receipt, Christina pinged his glass of scotch, sending ripples through the amber liquid. "Are you leaving this? By my calculations, that's about eight bucks sitting in that glass, eight bucks the Bureau isn't paying for."

"I'm good. Do you want the rest?"

She wrinkled her nose. "Only if you toss it in with some sweet liqueurs and mixers and stick a colorful umbrella in it."

"Uh, no." He folded the receipt and stuck it in his pocket. "Are you ready?"

"Kindred Spirits is around the corner." She picked up her phone and tipped it back and forth. "Open until midnight on Friday night."

"Let's go inhale some incense."

He placed his hand on the small of her back and steered her out of the crowded restaurant.

As they passed their car on the street, Eric fed a few more quarters into the meter. "You don't want to stick the Bureau with a parking ticket."

She rolled her eyes. "Do you really think they'd pay for my parking ticket?"

"Even more reason not to get one." He slipped another quarter into the slot.

They turned the corner and he dipped his head against the sharp wind that whipped around the building. Even during the summer, the San Francisco Bay kept the city cool. "Is it on this block or the next one?"

Holding up her phone, she answered, "It's actually in an alley off this street."

They walked about halfway down the sidewalk, and Christina jerked her thumb to the right. "Down here."

The alley dropped two steps and the ground beneath their feet changed to cobblestones. Music wafted or blared from the storefronts, depending on the wares inside. A wooden sign with Kindred Spirits printed in red along with a bubbling cauldron creaked in front of one of the stores.

He tugged on a wayward lock of Christina's long hair. "That's our store."

"Cute logo." She tapped the edge of the sign as they ducked into the store.

The top of his head brushed a tassel of bells hanging from the doorway and their light tinkle announced their arrival.

Soft New Age music played in the background and Eric's nose twitched at the smell of sandalwood incense. He sniffed. "Told you so."

"Smells nice."

A woman emerged from the back of the store, throwing one impossibly long gray braid over her shoulder. "Welcome, kindred spirits. Can I help you with something, or are you here to browse?"

Eric pressed his twitching lips into a hard line. "We're actually here to ask you a couple of questions about a former employee, Nora Sterling. We're with the FBI. I'm Agent Brody, and this is Agent Sandoval."

Shaking her head, the woman placed her hands together as if in prayer. She mumbled a few words between barely moving lips.

He took a quick glance at Christina, but she refused to meet his eyes. "Excuse me?"

"A very sad situation." The woman lowered her hands. "But the police already came in here asking questions."

"We're not the police." Christina took a few steps through the crowded store toward the woman and thrust out her hand. "And you are?"

"Libby Rivers. I'm the owner of the…" She had taken Christina's hand and then jerked, almost flinging Christina's hand away.

Christina took a step back. "A-are you okay?"

"I'm sorry. A little static electricity." She smoothed her hand along the length of her braid. "As I was saying, I'm the owner of the store and Nora worked for me."

Eric drew his brows together. Christina was staring at the woman, rubbing her palm against the thigh of her jeans.

"I'd shake your hand, too, but I don't want to shock you." He plucked a green marble from a glass bowl and rolled it in his palm. "Can you tell us anything about Nora? Did she have visitors to the store? Complain about anyone stalking her? Have any unusual interactions with a customer?"

Libby flicked her fingers. "The police already asked me all of that."

"It's different talking to someone in person and reading someone else's notes."

"What do you really want, Agent Brody?"

He blinked. Were his questioning skills that bad? He reached into the front pocket of his jeans and pulled out the piece of notepaper with the symbol. He snapped it open and turned it toward Libby. "What does this mean?"

Libby's faded blue eyes flickered. "Where did you see that?"

"Can't tell you that, Libby." He waved the paper under her nose. "What does it mean?"

She snatched it from his hand and pressed it against her

chest, right above her heart. "It's the symbol of a coven, Agent Brody."

He folded his arms. "A coven? You mean like a coven of witches?"

"There's a war going on, Agent Brody, a war against this coven."

Then she dropped the paper and her hand shot out, and she grabbed Christina's wrist, pulling her closer. "And that includes you, Agent Sandoval."

Chapter Five

Libby's cool blue eyes burned into Christina's face. The clawlike fingers dug into her flesh.

Eric shifted beside her, sucking in his breath, automatically reaching for his weapon.

Christina stumbled back a step and wrenched her arm away from Libby's grip. "What are you talking about?"

"I'm sorry." Libby coiled her braid around one hand. "Did I frighten you? That's good. You should be frightened."

Eric squared his shoulders and stepped between them. "Are you threatening her?"

"Me?" Libby backed up and bent over, sweeping the paper with the symbol from the floor as her long braid fell over one shoulder. "I'm not the one your partner has to look out for, Agent Brody."

"Who, then? Why should I be afraid of a war on this coven, and what exactly do you mean by a war?"

Libby clicked her tongue. "You're one of those who denies her powers. Stuffs them away. Ignores them. But you're one of us, Agent Sandoval."

"Did you just call me a witch?" Christina tried for a light tone, but Libby didn't crack a smile. How did the woman know about her special powers? That handshake—something had passed between them.

"Whether you belong to this coven," she said, tapping the symbol, "or another, you're still a witch."

"Okay, maybe there's a little ESP going on here, someone with special gifts sensing it in someone else, but I'm no witch and I certainly didn't join any coven." She pointed to the piece of paper Libby had placed on the counter. "This one or any other."

"You don't join a coven, my dear. You belong." Libby turned to Eric. "Nora did. She belonged to this coven."

Eric whistled. "Did she, umm, practice witchcraft?"

"She did." Libby's gaze trailed to Christina. "There are some who embrace their powers."

Christina dug her high heels into the floor. "Do you have any proof that Nora was murdered because she belonged to this coven?"

"Tell me. Did you find the sign of this coven on Nora?" Libby reached into a drawer and pulled out three incense sticks. "Or someone else?"

Eric shot her a look and cleared his throat. "We can't tell you that, Libby."

She nodded. "Someone else. So now you have two victims who are tied to this coven. Are you going to tell me that the coven isn't the common denominator here?"

The bells over the door shivered and they all jerked their heads up. A tall man, dressed all in black with a black fedora, filled the doorway and for a second Christina had an urge to flee.

Libby folded the sheet of paper with the symbol and slid it toward Eric. "Hello, Nigel. More patchouli oil?"

"It's a little more serious than that, Libby. I need a new deck of cards."

Christina weaved her fingers through Eric's and tightened her hold.

"I knew that was coming." She waved her hand over Christina and Eric as if sprinkling fairy dust…or casting a spell. "This is Agent Brody and Agent Sandoval with the FBI. They're looking into Nora's murder."

Nigel tipped back his hat. "Sick bastard. Nora was a sweet girl."

Eric's frame tensed. "You knew her?"

"From the store." He held up a crooked finger. "Brody. Are you related to the SFPD homicide detective?"

Eric clenched his jaw so tightly Christina was afraid it would snap.

"He's my brother."

"Which one of you was kidnapped?"

Libby expelled a breath and it turned into a hiss.

"What do you know about that?" Eric shook off her hand and clenched his into a fist.

"Easy, boy. I'm a native. I know the city's history, lore and legends better than most. Who could forget Joseph Brody's story? Son kidnapped in the middle of a serial killer investigation? It was all a sensation." He tapped his head. "I don't forget anything that happened in this city."

Libby rapped a deck of cards on the counter. "Your tarot cards, Nigel."

"Tarot cards?" Christina held out her hand. "Can I see them?"

"You don't need them. They're more for the wannabes." Libby fluttered her gray lashes in what could be a wink but dropped the cards in Christina's hand. "Sorry, Nigel."

Christina spread out the cards on the table, studying each one for similarities with the power and death cards found at the crime scenes. She located the two cards, but they were from a different tarot deck than these. "Do you sell a lot of tarot decks?"

The blue eyes turned to slits. "I sell my fair share, but people can order them online. Why?"

"Just curious." Christina scooped up the cards and

handed them to Nigel, avoiding his touch. She didn't need another secret witch handshake right now.

His dark eyes bore into her anyway. "Are you close to finding Nora's killer?"

Eric poked her in the back and she shrugged away from him. Did he take her for a rookie?

"We'll get him." She formed her fingers into a gun and pulled the trigger.

Nigel slipped the cards into his pocket and pulled out a silver money clip. "How much do I owe you, Libby?"

She tapped a few keys on her register. "Thirty-seven dollars and forty-two cents."

He pulled two twenties from the clip, took his change and limped toward the door, his gray hair sticking out from the brim of his fedora.

He paused and raised one hand. "Find the people who are doing this."

Christina blew out a breath when he disappeared. "Is he a witch, too?"

"No, but he's good with the cards." Libby patted Eric's arm. "Sorry if Nigel made you uncomfortable, Agent Brody. Your father's case riveted the city back in the day, and it all came back when the Alphabet Killer started leaving messages for your brother a few months ago."

"Jesus." Eric raked a hand through his hair. "You know all about my family, too?"

She shrugged. "Like Nigel said, it was a sensational case."

"Do you remember my kidnapping?"

"Of course, but when you walked in here and introduced yourself, I didn't realize you were the brother who had been kidnapped."

"I don't see how my brother can put up with this, living here."

"People forget, move on to the next tragedy. It's just

fresh in our minds because of the recent case. Nobody really believed your father killed those women."

Eric's chest rose and fell. "He jumped from the bridge."

Libby twirled her braid. "Lots of people jump from the bridge."

Christina raised her voice and tilted her chin toward the door. "Any reason to suspect Nigel?"

Libby chuckled. "Nigel can barely turn those tarot cards his arthritis is so bad. He's not capable of wrapping his hands around a knife and slitting someone's throat."

"Is there anything else you can tell us, Libby?"

She raised her delicate brows. "Haven't I told you enough? I gave you the motive."

Eric snorted. "A war on witches? What for?"

"Dominance, power."

Christina's ears perked up. Had Libby noticed her special attention to the power card in the tarot deck, or did she really know something?

"Did you think I meant a bunch of God-fearing Christians were waging this war against the coven?" Libby tsked. "It's not outsiders, Agent Brody. It's another coven of witches. Mark my word."

When they hit the sidewalk, Christina gulped in the fresh air. "Did we just enter an alternate universe, or what?"

"I felt like we were the ones being interrogated in there. Libby knew all about your witchiness and old Nigel knew all about my family history."

"Watch it." She punched him in the shoulder.

"What happened when she shook your hand? Some kind of witch-to-witch communication?"

"Would you stop calling me a witch?"

"Tea?" He nodded toward a coffeehouse at the end of the alley. "I need to process this."

"Sure." Her arm swept along the street and the people

strolling from shop to shop. "Apparently the night's still young here in The Haight."

"You haven't been away from city life that long, have you?" He opened the door for her.

"They do roll up the sidewalks in San Miguel at ten o'clock on Friday nights, eight on weeknights."

"You loved the city. Why'd you move out?"

"Ah, I thought I told you. My mom needed some help." She folded her arms and peered at the drink menu on the wall.

"You told me your mom had retired from nursing. You're *living* with her?"

"Mom and I always got along, sort of."

"Is she really ill?"

"Small chai latte, please." She shook her head. "Just slowing down a bit, and she likes the company."

"That's why I'm surprised she retired." He ordered a decaf coffee, and they took a table in the corner.

He shifted in the wood chair and stretched his legs in front of him. "Did you know anything about witches' covens before Libby gave us the 411?"

"You mean anything other than what I've seen in the movies?" She popped the lid from her cup and blew on the surface. "My half sister's a witch."

Eric sputtered and wiped the coffee from his chin. "Vivi's a witch?"

"I thought I told you that before, too."

"You must be having imaginary conversations in your head with me because you never put it that way before. I thought she just dabbled in the occult." He blotted beads of coffee off the table with a napkin. "What does that mean exactly, that she's a witch? Does she cast spells and mix potions?"

"I've never gotten into it that much with her. She tried to

drag me into the occult when she found out I had certain…
sensitivities, but I shut her down."

"Must be a genetic thing from your—dad?"

"Yes, dear old dad is a powerful brujo."

"Okay, wait a minute." He splayed his hands on the table
and hunched forward. "I *know* you never told me that. I
thought your dad was a musician who told fortunes."

"He's a musician *and* a brujo."

"Is that why he and your mom divorced?"

"Oh, it was one of many issues." She sipped her tea and
then wrapped her hands around the warm cup. "He was
all in favor of developing my psychic talents, but Mom put
the brakes on that."

"Wow." Eric tapped his chin with his fingertips. "It's
weird that you got this case."

She snapped her brows together. "Why is it weird? I'm
working serial killers in the West. We've got a serial killer
in the West."

He smoothed his thumb across the back of her hand.
"I'm just saying. It's a coincidence."

"Like it's a coincidence that Liz Fielding was wearing
the same necklace and may be a member of the same coven
as the woman who was involved in your kidnapping?"

His thumb stopped its circular motion on her hand.
"What are you saying? Like you mentioned before, I'm
working serial killers in the Western Division, and here
we are."

"Maybe it's some force at work." Her hands encom-
passed a ball in the air. "Maybe we're meant to work this
case—together."

"Then let's do it." He encircled her wrists with his fingers. "Tell me what you know about witches and covens."

"I wish I knew more. My mother told me that people
used to come and see Dad for help, mostly communicating
with dead relatives. He acted as a medium."

"You were too young to see any of this, right?"

"Oh, yeah. Dad left before I was five."

"He remarried?"

"No."

"Your half sister?"

"My father's a musician and a brujo. He didn't need marriage to procreate."

"So he handed down his gifts to another daughter? One whose mother didn't mind the development of the talent?"

"Mind? She may have encouraged it. There are a few women who would seek out a brujo just for that purpose."

"To have a baby with him?"

She nodded over the steam rising from her cup.

"What kind of woman would use a baby as a pawn?"

Christina coughed. "You can never understand other people's motives."

"Seems pretty low to me."

"Anyway," she continued, tapping the table as if to bring his focus back, "that's about all I know. I'm not sure what kind of witchcraft Vivi practices."

Eric sketched out the symbol on a napkin. "Do you think she's in the same coven as Nora and Liz?"

"I don't know, but what about your guy in San Diego and the other woman in Portland?"

"We're going to have to comb through the files and look for the link. We weren't looking at witchcraft, were we?"

"Nope. We got our break tonight."

He drained his cup. "Let's call it a night and see if we can link the other two murders to this coven. Where is your father, anyway?"

"Mexico. Why? Did you think you could use him for research?"

"Where's Vivi?"

"Great. You're going to try to question her? I think she's in Big Sur."

"We can always make a return trip to Kindred Spirits."

"One thing at a time. We need to make sure this theory applies to the other two victims, or we're dead in the water."

"I have a feeling about this one."

"Now that makes two of us with feelings. We should open our own detective agency."

"And compete with my little brother, Judd?"

"Ah, but does Judd have *feelings?*"

He snorted. "He actually has very few of those."

"Let's head back. I'm really curious to look at those case files now."

Tossing his half-full coffee cup into the trash, he asked, "We are going to bed first, right?"

Her eyes flew to his face, but shadows obscured his expression, so she shrugged off the double entendre. "I plan to get a good night's sleep. I know I have to look at those files with fresh eyes."

"Now we have something specific to look for."

They stepped off the curb and a car engine revved. Her step faltered, and Eric jerked his head to the side. He held up his hand in case the guy behind the headlights wasn't paying attention.

As they entered the crosswalk, tires squealed and the car hurtled toward them.

Christina screamed and flew through the air.

Chapter Six

Eric still had her by the waist where he'd grabbed her just as the car whooshed past them, spewing exhaust and burning rubber into the air.

Several pedestrians shook their heads and one man yelled an obscenity after the speeding car.

Christina had stumbled back against Eric's chest, and he pulled her tightly against his body. "Are you okay?"

"That was close." Her voice shook and she cleared her throat. "What's the matter with that guy? Didn't he see us?"

"He saw us, Christina."

She spun around, her nose almost touching his. "Are you sure?"

"I waved at him. Didn't you hear the car take off? Zero to fifty."

"Okay, what are you saying, Eric?" She placed her hands on his solid chest and leaned away from him. "Do you think he was aiming for us?"

"Sure seems that way."

Her fingers curled around the fabric of his shirt. "Then it's no coincidence. I know there are some bad drivers in this city, but they usually don't aim for pedestrians."

"Unless those pedestrians are investigating a series of murders and are getting too close for comfort."

Her heart pounded in her chest and her breath came out in short spurts. "That's crazy. We're the FBI for God's sake."

"Do you think that exempts us from people taking potshots at us? We just lost an agent in South America. Someone blew his cover and the cartel executed him, beheaded him."

She shivered and hugged her waist. "Nothing like this has ever happened to me before."

"Me either." He grabbed her hand. "Let's get back to the car. We don't want to give him a second chance."

"Do you think it's our killer? Do you think he plans to strike again in San Francisco?"

"I hope he tries and we're there to stop him this time."

"We need to report this to Rich."

"We have no proof that the guy driving that car has anything to do with this case."

"There's the symbol on my rental car. Someone's following us, someone who's aware we're here to investigate these murders."

"I'll put it in my report to Rich and the P.D." He held out his hand. "Do you want me to drive? Your hands are trembling."

She dropped the keys into his palm without a word. If he wanted to play the big strong protector, who was she to argue?

When she slid into the passenger seat, she leaned back to get a view of the side mirror. "I'm going to make sure we're not being followed."

"Why? That would be great. Let him come to us."

"Easy for you to say. Those weren't your toes he almost ran over with a two-ton car."

Drawing his brows together, he adjusted the rearview mirror. "Did you feel like he was aiming the car toward you? We were both in that crosswalk."

"I don't know. Maybe just because I was in front of you. Scary stuff." She wriggled deeper into her seat and stuffed her hands beneath her thighs. Tonight had been a roller coaster ride. Maybe she should try to call Vivi and see what she had to say about the matter. Of course, every time she talked to her sister, Vivi tried to recruit her to the dark side.

"Are you okay?" Eric reached over and squeezed her shoulder.

"I'd be better if I thought the hot tub at the hotel would be open when we got back." He removed his hand too soon and steered into the hotel parking lot.

Despite being outed as a witch and almost getting run over, this night had exceeded all her expectations. Eric had forgiven her for taking secret notes on his family tragedy and didn't believe she'd been in league with Ray Lopez to write a book. He'd softened toward her, and it felt so good she'd almost forgotten that she had a bigger secret—one that would torpedo their tentative truce.

But she had to tell him.

He parked the car, and she scrambled out before she could blurt out the truth. This needed careful planning. He was already suspicious about her move to San Miguel with her mother. Mom was hardly old or sickly.

She blinked as they walked into the glare of the lobby.

Eric called across the room to the hotel clerk. "Is the hot tub still open?"

She responded. "Midnight."

"Perfect." Eric took her arm. "The witching hour."

"Would you stop with that?" She shook off his hand. "I already told you. Midnight is not the witching hour."

"Like I said, you should know." He punched the elevator button. "Are you really going to the hot tub? Did you even bring a suit?"

"I always do."

They reached their adjoining rooms, and she slid her

card in the slot and turned, but he already had his own door open.

"I'll see you at breakfast tomorrow morning at eight?"

"Sure."

The stab of disappointment almost took her breath away. Not that she was expecting a good-night kiss or anything, but something more than a door in the face would've been nice after their breakthrough tonight.

She let her own door slam behind her. Maybe Eric didn't consider what had happened tonight a breakthrough.

And it wasn't. The breakthrough would come when she told him about Kendall. Or not.

After she tugged on her one-piece suit, she crouched in front of the minibar and grabbed a mini bottle of chilled white wine. She didn't have to drive anywhere now.

She slipped the white terry cloth robe from the hanger in the closet and wrapped it around her body. She dropped the wine in her pocket, followed by a plastic cup. She padded barefoot down the carpeted hallway to the elevator. She stabbed the button for the basement floor a couple of times.

She slid her key card into the slot next to the glass door leading to the pool. She nodded at the couple dog-paddling around the shallow end. Probably thrilled to see her.

Steam rose from the hot tub, which was tucked in the corner of the room and she cruised toward it, shedding her robe along the way.

A head stuck up above the edge, and she tripped to a stop. Awkward. She was hoping to have it to herself. Maybe he'd leave.

As she approached the enclosure, the person in the hot tub turned his head and she almost tripped again.

"Took you long enough." Eric sat up straight and the hot water sluiced from his broad shoulders and steam rose from his back.

She had to snap her mouth shut and just hope no drool had made it to her chin. "You."

He ran a hand across his hair, and his biceps bunched. "Sounded like a good idea. Hop in. It's nice and hot."

She had to peel her tongue from the roof of her mouth to speak and she still managed only a gurgle.

She entered the enclosure and dipped a toe into the bubbling water. "Yep, it's hot."

Eric lifted one corner of his mouth, and the heat spread to her cheeks. Idiot.

She stepped into the tub and sank onto the tile seat across from him. Her foot touched his and she jerked it back. His presence here did not bode well for a relaxing soak.

Sighing, she scooted farther into the water and rested the back of her head on the edge of the pool. She shifted so that the jets pounded between her shoulder blades. "Ahh."

He lowered his body back beneath the surface of the frothing water. "Feels good. Thanks for the suggestion. Hope you don't mind."

"Not at all. It's a good way to unwind after work. Beats booze."

"Apparently not." He pointed to the little bottle of wine perched on the deck with the plastic cup snug over the top.

"I—I…just a little nightcap."

"Christina," he said as he cupped some water in his hand and tipped it over, "you don't have to pretend to be a teetotaler for me. I ordered two drinks at dinner, remember?"

"I know. It's just that your mom…"

"Was an alcoholic and a prescription drug addict. That was my mom. I don't put a black check mark next to someone's name just because they like a social drink now and then."

"I know. It's silly." To prove her point, she grabbed the bottle and twisted off the cap.

"A twist cap? Only the best, huh?"

She turned the bottle in her hand and studied the dark blue label. "It's actually a decent chardonnay from a good little winery in Sonoma—not that I would know one from the other."

"Of course not. Leave a little in the bottle for me. I'd like to try it."

She poured most of the golden liquid into the plastic cup, leaving a gulp for Eric.

"Here you go." She handed him the bottle through the steam, and it promptly beaded up with moisture.

He took it and tipped the neck toward her. "Here's to finding our guy."

"To finding our guy." She tapped the rim of her cup with the bottle and took a sip. The cool liquid ran down her throat, contrasting with the heat on her skin, made hotter by the man lounging across from her. "There is one hot tub rule I have to ask you to follow."

"What's that? No nudity?"

His grin melted her insides even more, and she splashed him. "That goes without saying. Those are the hotel rules, anyway. This is my personal rule for hot tub time."

"I'm listening." He wrapped his lips around the bottle and tipped his head back.

"No shoptalk. This is time to relax, not rehash."

"You got it." He touched the bottle to his forehead, and then aimed it at her chest. "You used to favor bikinis. What happened?"

She smothered a cough and almost snorted wine out of her nose. "I always like a one-piece at the hotel pools. Stays on better when I want to do a little swimming."

She'd just started feeling comfortable in a bikini after her pregnancy and giving birth to Kendall, but she couldn't explain that to Eric. This craziness had to stop. She couldn't continue to work with him and keep the most important part of her life a secret.

"Yeah, I guess I remember you always did wear a one-piece in the ocean."

She took another sip of wine and cupped its sweetness on her tongue before swallowing it. Was it time to get personal? "So you never came back to the city after South America?"

"They sent me to D.C. I've been homebasing it there."

"Do you miss the city? Your brothers?"

"Yes and sort of. I was kind of relieved when I found out Sean was on an extended vacation. He's so damned controlling."

"At least he's not a witch."

"Yeah, he's got that going for him." He made a cross over his heart and said, "Not to bring up work, but speaking of siblings, when is the last time you saw your sister Vivi?"

"About a month ago, but you know what's funny?"

"Besides your father being a brujo and your sister being a witch? What?"

"I had a dream about Vivi a few weeks ago."

"Good? Bad?"

She massaged her temple with her fingertips. "It just came to me. I had forgotten all about it."

"Do you remember what it was about?"

He had stretched out his legs and wedged his feet against her seat, too close to her thigh for comfort.

She scooted over a little. "I don't remember now. Just Vivi being Vivi, yapping up a storm about something. Maybe she was at the front of a classroom and I was a student. Something like that."

"Is she much younger than you? Five years?"

"About six. I think my father groomed her like he wanted to do with me had my mom allowed it."

"I think your mom made a wise decision."

"You think I should contact Vivi about this coven stuff, don't you?" She tucked a few damp tendrils of hair behind her ear.

He raised his shoulders out of the water. "Couldn't hurt, could it? Are you two on good terms?"

"Sure. She's a crazy kid, but she means well." Actually, they'd had an argument over Kendall the last time they'd seen each other. Vivi had gotten the nutty idea that they should test Kendall for psychic ability. A *baby*.

Of course, she couldn't reveal any of this to Eric, and if she did contact Vivi she'd have to keep her away from Eric so her sister wouldn't let the cat out of the bag. Her head began to pound with the thought of keeping her lies straight.

"I'll leave it up to you, and I promise I won't break the rule again, or at least that rule."

He pushed up with his arms and his body floated to the right. Shifting into position, he closed his eyes. "Right there. My lower back has been killing me."

The jets gurgled as the water shot against his back, and Christina's fingers tingled as she thought about digging them into his skin to relieve his pain as she'd done so many times before.

He used to tell her she had magic hands, better than any masseuse or chiropractor, but she knew her ability to relieve his pain had nothing to do with her talents and everything to do with love. Because she'd loved this man with every fiber of her being.

And still did.

"I have some ibuprofen in my room."

"That would help. It's that old football injury acting up. It was better on my previous assignment because I wasn't sitting at a desk so much."

The couple from the pool were making their way toward

the hot tub and Eric murmured under his breath. "Uh-oh. I hate communal hot tubs."

The woman put her foot on the first step. "Mind if we join you?"

"You can have it to yourselves." Christina stood up and the air caused a rash of goose pimples to rush across her skin. "We were getting ready to leave anyway."

Eric rose from the water looking like a Greek god. If that's the body he got from sitting in a chair too much, she'd like to patent that chair.

The other woman missed her step and splashed into the hot tub.

Eric caught her arm. "Careful."

She laughed. "Didn't even see that second step."

Christina's lip curled. *Yeah, because you were staring at my man.*

Her possessive feelings toward Eric punched her in the gut. This case was going to take a toll on her in more ways than one. What had Rich been thinking putting the two of them together?

She bent at the knees to snatch up her cup and then tossed it in the trash can. She toweled off and draped her body in the oversize robe.

Eric stuffed the wine bottle into the trash and swiped his towel across his back and then flung it over one shoulder. "Ready?"

"Do you still want that ibuprofen?"

"Yep. The jets helped but not as much as—other things."

Was he thinking about her magic hands? All he had to do was say the word and she'd be all over him.

She crooked her finger. "Follow me."

"Anywhere."

They rode up the elevator in silence. Was he struggling as much as she was? And what was his struggle? Trust?

Telling him he'd been a father the past two years wouldn't do much to alleviate that.

When they reached their rooms, they both swiped their cards.

He pointed into his room. "I'll meet you at the secret door."

She closed her door and scooped in a deep breath. She needed to delve down for some willpower. She couldn't start getting cozy with Eric and then drop the A-bomb on him, or in this case, the *P*-bomb for *parenthood.*

She clicked her card down on the credenza and reached for her purse. She dug inside for her little bottle of ibuprofen and pulled out her phone at the same time to charge it.

The knock on the adjoining door made her almost drop both phone and bottle.

"Yeah, I got it." She crossed the room and turned the dead bolt. He'd better use the one on his side, too, since she didn't trust herself in the middle of the night sleeping alone in a cold bed.

He eased open the door. "Everyone decent?"

"Nothing you haven't seen before." She opened her robe and spread her arms.

The way his hazel eyes sparked to green as they traveled over her body, made it seem as if he were seeing her for the first time.

She shook the pills in the bottle, and then tossed it at him. "Here you go."

With his quick reflexes, he swiped a hand through the air and caught the bottle with a snap. He thumbed up the lid. "I'm going to steal your water, too, since you already have a bottle open."

"My wine, my painkillers, my water. What else are you going to steal from me?"

Someone banged on her hotel door, and this time she did drop her phone.

"Wait." Eric stepped into her room and headed for her door just as the banging started again. He looked through the peephole. He motioned her over. "Do you know this guy?"

She huddled in next to him and looked through the peephole. She whispered, "No."

Once more, the young man with slicked-back black hair pummeled his fists against the door. "Hello? Anyone in there? Christina Sandoval? I'm Vivi's friend."

Christina took a step back, turning wide eyes on Eric and lifting her shoulders.

"Vivi's missing, and I'm afraid she might be in danger."

Chapter Seven

Christina swayed, and she clutched on to Eric like a lifeline.

Eric reached past her and swung open the door. "Who are you?"

The man jerked back. "I—I'm Darius Cole, Vivi Sandoval's friend."

"How the hell did you know Christina was staying here?"

The man's pale skin blanched even further. "She told me. Vivi told me her sister was in the city and staying at this hotel."

Eric glanced at her, and she spread her hands. When she talked to Vivi last month, she'd mentioned coming to the city to work and had probably mentioned her hotel. What did it matter now? She brushed past Eric and grabbed Darius's arm, dragging him into the room. "Tell me what happened. How long has Vivi been missing?"

"Two weeks." He jerked out of her grasp. "You're some kind of cop, right? Vivi told us."

"FBI. Have you called the police?"

"They won't listen." Darius made a circle around the room, clenching his hands, his black boots clumping on the floor. "They said she's an adult and there's nothing they can do without evidence of foul play, or something like that."

"Okay, calm down."

Christina squeezed her eyes closed, feeling anything but calm herself, and then Eric was next to her rubbing a circle on her back. She dropped her shoulders and took a deep breath. "Start from the beginning. Is—was Vivi still in Big Sur?"

"Santa Cruz. We were all staying at Papa Bud's house."

"Papa Bud?" She raised her brows at Eric.

Darius flicked long white fingers. "He's just a guy in Santa Cruz, has a big house and everyone's welcome."

"How long have you and Vivi been staying there?"

"A few months. We'd been working near the boardwalk. I've been bartending and Vivi's been reading the cards, telling fortunes."

"Did she say anything before she left? Meet up with anyone? What about this Papa Bud?"

"Papa Bud's cool. He's just as worried as the rest of us."

"Was Vivi using drugs there?"

"Not much, a little weed." He shrugged. "You know Vivi. She can reach an alternate state all on her own. She doesn't need any help."

"So what were the circumstances of her departure? Did she take her purse, her car?"

"We didn't have a car at the time. We hitched a ride down the coast to see some people and then came up to the city where I had my car and were planning to go back down to Santa Cruz. That's when she took off. She took her purse and one bag."

A trickle of relief meandered through her body and she slumped against Eric, whose arm had found its way around her waist. "It sounds to me like she just got tired of Papa Bud's and telling fortunes on the boardwalk. If you know Vivi, you know she's always looking for new experiences."

He ran his hands through his dark hair, making it stand up even more. "That's why the cops won't do anything. They think she just took off on her own."

"And you don't?"

"She didn't say anything to anyone. She just stole away in the middle of the night. Why would she do that?" Darius nibbled on a fingernail that he'd painted black.

She rolled her eyes at Eric. "Did she owe someone money?"

"No, but she was worried about something."

Christina's pulse ticked up again. "Did she tell you what?"

"I'm not sure, but I think it had something to do with those murders."

"What murders?"

Eric's arm tightened around her and she was glad of it.

"She had newspaper clippings of a murder in San Diego and another one in Portland—one man and one woman."

"Did she say anything about them?" Christina licked her lips and shot a sideways glance at Eric.

"Not much, but she kept the articles and read them so much they became dog-eared. And she seemed frightened. Santa Cruz is pretty laid-back, but she wouldn't stay at the boardwalk once the sun went down."

"Do you know if anyone was stalking or threatening her?"

"In Santa Cruz?"

"Look, I know you think Santa Cruz is paradise on earth, but there are a lot of crazies there just like anywhere else. Maybe one of her clients, someone who saw her on the boardwalk started fixating on her or something."

"Why wouldn't she just tell us? And we'd already left the boardwalk. Why take off all secretive like that?"

"We're talking about Vivi here. Your guess is as good as mine."

"You don't care about your sister? You don't want to find her?"

Christina's body stiffened and Eric's hand moved to the

back of her neck and squeezed. "Of course I do, but you haven't given me anything. What do you think happened to her? If someone abducted her, why would she take her purse and pack a bag?"

"She packed a bag, but she left her most important possessions."

"What would that be, her bong?"

Darius whistled. "Wow, you really are a cop, aren't you?"

"Just tell me what she left that was so important to her."

"Her tarot cards, her incense, her amulet."

"Her amulet?"

Darius tapped his throat. "A necklace she always wore. Why would she leave that stuff?"

Eric snapped his fingers and strode across the floor to his own room, calling over his shoulder. "What did Vivi's necklace look like?"

"It's a circle with two wavy lines and then a straight line intersecting the wavy lines."

As Darius described the amulet, Eric returned to her room waving the notepaper with the symbol of Liz Fielding's necklace. "Like this?"

"Whoa, man. Where'd you get that?" Darius snatched the paper from Eric. "That's it."

Christina covered her mouth with one hand. What did it mean? Was Vivi a member of this coven, too? "I—I've never seen her wear that."

"Well, she did, all the time, under her clothes. And she left it. Why would she leave that and the other stuff?"

Because someone is killing off members of her coven.

"I'm not sure, Darius. Look, just keep me posted. I think Vivi left of her own free will. I don't think you need to worry."

He held the paper back out to Eric. "You're not going to tell me where you got that drawing?"

"FBI business." Eric shoved the paper into the pocket of his damp trunks.

Christina took a deep breath. "She'll probably be in touch later, and I'll keep you posted."

"Here's my number." Darius hunched over the nightstand and scribbled on the hotel notepad. "I hope you're right. She thinks a lot of her big sister."

Unexpected moisture pooled in her eyes, and her nose tingled. "I'm sure she's fine. She probably just wanted a break. Take care of her cards and necklace. Put them away. Put the necklace away. She'll be back."

"You'll let me know as soon as you find her?" Darius crossed his muscular arms and took a stance like he wasn't leaving until she agreed.

"Yes. I'll let you know." She held out her hand. "Thanks for coming by and telling me all this."

Darius unfolded his arms but didn't take her hand, leveling a finger at her instead. "Just find her. I think she's in danger."

"I'll do my best."

Darius stepped toward the door Eric was holding open and shook his hand before he slipped out.

Christina stared at the closed door.

"Are you okay?" Eric's low voice brought her back from an abyss of crazy.

She turned her head, widened her eyes and sank to the bed. "What do you think is going on? Tell me before I go off the deep end here."

"I think," he murmured, flicking a damp lock of hair from her shoulder, "something or someone was threatening your sister and she decided to hightail it out of Santa Cruz and Papa Bud's commune. She made a stop in the city with that hippie bodybuilder and then didn't feel safe, so she took off."

"And she left her stuff, the tools of her trade, her witchy

accoutrements. Why?" She spread her hands as if hoping to find the answer in the lines crisscrossing her palms.

"Isn't it clear? She doesn't want to be associated with the tools of her trade. She doesn't want to be identified as a witch."

Christina puffed out a breath. "It sounds more sensible when you say it, but that's exactly what I was thinking."

"What did Libby say?"

"There's a war against witches." She bounded up from the bed and paced the floor, threading her fingers in front of her. "How do you think the Bureau is going to react when we hand them this motive for the killings?"

"Do you think they'll be less interested just because the victims are witches?" He fell onto his side and propped up his head with his hand, his elbow digging into the bed—her bed.

"No. I don't know. Rich will think we're nuts. He'll think I'm making things up."

"Proof is proof. Evidence is evidence."

"We don't have much of either." She stopped beside the bed and rested her knee on top of it. "What are the chances that my own sister is involved in this?"

"She's not involved, Christina." He rolled to his back and crossed his hands behind his head.

"She obviously knows what's going on. She knows she's a target."

"That's a good thing, and we have a good starting point here. Libby mentioned another coven. I say we do a little research…tomorrow."

"You're right. I just wish I didn't have to worry about Vivi on top of everything else I'm worried about."

He sat up and cocked his head. "What else are you worried about?"

She nibbled on her lower lip. Eric Brody sprawled across

her bed, for one thing. And continuing to lie to him about their daughter for another.

She closed her eyes to block out the vision of him, still in his trunks, lounging on her bed.

Bad idea. She felt his warm breath on her cheek as he rose from the mattress and took her hand.

"Your sister's going to be fine, Christina. Whoever drew that symbol on your windshield and blew past you in the car is just playing games, and if he isn't, if he means you harm," he said as he wedged a finger beneath her chin, "he's going to have to get through me first."

She blinked. She'd honestly forgotten about her newly acquired stalker, but she could do a lot worse than having Eric in her corner. She never thought she'd be able to say that again.

She curved her lips into a smile. "Thanks. That makes me feel warm and fuzzy."

"Are you being sarcastic?" He pinched her chin.

"I'm serious. I—I'm glad you're here, Eric."

"I am, too, and I'll be right next door all night if you need anything or if you have any bad dreams."

"You know I probably had that dream about Vivi around the same time she took off. She was communicating with me."

"You're probably right."

She searched his face for any hint of humor, but saw only concern. That's what she'd always loved about Eric— he was a tough guy with an empathetic soul. He'd had enough tragedy in his young life to be able to truly feel what others felt.

His hazel eyes darkened to bottle-green, and she parted her lips. He brushed his mouth against hers so quickly, she might have imagined it.

"Call me if you need me. I'm leaving my side of the door unlocked tonight." He waved his hand in the air.

"But I am closing it. Apparently, Darius likes nail polish *and* perfume."

She nodded stupidly and stared at his broad, bare back as he headed into his own room.

Eric clicked the door shut, and then smacked his forehead with his palm.

He had no self-control. A kiss? It's not like she was falling apart at the seams. Christina Sandoval did not fall apart at the seams. She didn't even have seams.

A sniffle. A teary eye. That's as far as it went with Agent Sandoval. She didn't even seem remotely bothered by the recent threats to her. She seemed strangely removed from those threats. Something else had her going—jumpy, tentative. Something more than her sister, since she'd been acting jittery ever since he walked into the station this morning.

With the way they'd left things between them, she had every right to be jittery. He'd been an ass.

He peeled off his damp board shorts and tossed them into the bathtub. Then he brushed his teeth and crawled naked between the sheets.

As he stared at the blinking green light on the smoke detector, he heard a click. He jerked his head toward the door between his room and Christina's.

"Damn." He'd forgotten his promise to her to leave the door unlocked on his side. He rolled from the bed and padded across the floor. Pressing one hand against the door, he turned the dead bolt. The click sounded like a gunshot.

He held his breath. Then he turned and crept back to bed. As his head hit the pillow, he heard an answering click from the other side of the door.

Was that an invitation?

He pulled the pillow over his head. *If you know what's good for you, Brody, ignore it.*

But when it came to Christina, that advice was easier said than done.

Chapter Eight

Christina greeted him in the hotel restaurant with heavy eyes and a yawn.

"You look like you need another eight hours of sleep."

"*Another* eight hours? Try two."

"Are you still worried about Vivi?"

"Yeah, Vivi." She dropped into the chair across from him and gulped down some of his ice water.

"I'll tell you what." He reached for his phone. "I'll give Judd a call and see if he can track her down."

"Would he do that?"

"If he's not busy." He scrolled through the contacts on his personal phone until he reached Judd's number. He tapped the phone and it rang on the other end.

His brother's gruff voice rumbled over the phone. "Judd Brody, leave a message."

"Judd, it's Eric. Give me a call. I want you to find someone for me."

He shook his head. "I don't see how that guy can make a living with his social skills."

"Do you think he'll call you back?"

"Like I said, if he's not on a case taking pics of some cheating spouse."

"Is that usually the type of work he does?" She wrinkled her nose.

"He'll take just about anything, but he does missing persons, a lot of bodyguarding, too."

"Any celebrities?"

"Here and there." He raised his brows. "Why? Are you thinking of writing another book?"

"Another book?" She smacked the table. "I thought we cleared that up? There was no book."

He patted her hand. "Take it easy. I was kidding. Is it too early to kid about that?"

"No, kid away. I'd rather have the bad jokes than the dagger looks." She waved at the waitress. "That reminds me. I still have those notes. I meant what I said then and now, Eric. Those notes are yours."

"I don't know what I'd do with them now."

"You used to be interested in finding out the truth about your father."

"I still am."

The waitress stopped at their table, and he ordered an omelet with the works while Christina settled for a bowl of oatmeal with berries.

She planted her elbows on the table and buried her chin in one palm. "What? You're not interested in your dad's case anymore?"

"Sean discovered something recently when he was investigating that Alphabet Killer."

"Something about your father?"

"When the Phone Book Killer started communicating with my father, the department recommended that he see a shrink."

"That makes sense—standard operating procedure for a lot of departments."

"Sean thought the psychiatrist might have some insight into my father's suicide, so he tracked down the doctor."

Christina hunched over the table, clasping her hands in front of her. "That's exciting."

"Didn't end up that way. The guy dropped dead minutes before Sean got there to question him."

"What?" She pushed her hair off her face, her eyes wide. "What happened?"

"He had a heart attack."

"Oh, my God. What are the chances of that happening?"

"Exactly."

"What does Sean think?"

"He thinks the doc may have had some information for him, information someone didn't want him to have."

"Does he have any proof that the heart attack was induced?"

"That's when he called me in, but I couldn't get a toxicology report on the doctor. We don't know what happened to him. It could've just been a heart attack. Maybe he got stressed-out thinking about my father's case and that brought on the attack."

"That's so strange."

The waitress dropped off their food, and Eric dug into his omelet. He pointed his fork at her bowl of mush. "Is that going to be enough?"

"Are you kidding? I've got brown sugar, bananas, berries. I'm in heaven."

"This," he said, waving his fork with a string of orange cheese hanging off it, "is heaven. Anyway, enough of my father's case. We have our own killer to find."

"We'll fire up your laptop and do a little research on covens."

"Maybe we can get more info from Libby. We should drop in on her again."

"Maybe we'll get lucky and Nigel will be around."

"So many witches, so little time." He stuffed another bite of omelet into his mouth.

They finished their breakfast, and took the elevator back up to their rooms. In the light of day, Eric felt more in control of his impulses. He wouldn't rule out another go around with Christina, but he wanted to make sure she wasn't harboring any more secrets.

He did believe that she never intended to write that book, but she'd kept her relationship with Ray Lopez a secret from him, and there was no doubt in his mind that if Lopez had gotten his hands on those notes, a book on his father dredging up the whole sordid affair would've been forthcoming.

Christina still had something to prove to him, and maybe he had something to prove to her, too.

Maybe that's why she was still skittish. She was just waiting for his moody psycho side to make another appearance.

The elevator dinged, bringing him out of his daydreams.

"My room?" She tapped on the door with her card.

"I'll meet you through the secret door, since I have the laptop."

"I have a laptop, too."

"Mine's faster."

She sighed. "If you insist. I'll meet you at the secret door, but you have to do the secret knock."

She twirled around and shut her door in his face.

In his room, he swept his computer from the table and knocked on the door that separated their rooms. "Ready?"

She flung the door open. "You got the secret knock right on the first try."

"I'm psychic." He wiggled his fingers in the air.

"Water?"

"Line 'em up." He set the laptop on the table by the window and powered it on. "Okay, what should we search for first? Covens?"

"Give it a try."

His hands hovered over the keyboard. "Do the covens actually have names?"

"I have no idea. Libby wasn't very forthcoming with the particulars."

"And your sister? Did she ever mention a name?"

"No. I never even knew she was a member of a coven. Her or my father. I didn't know there were different covens."

"Maybe they're like sororities. You have to rush a coven and they make sure you're a good fit." He tapped a few keys.

She stuck out her tongue. "Don't be dumb. Remember what Libby said? You don't join a coven, you just are."

He ignored the tongue and stared so hard at the screen, his vision blurred. "I'm wondering if half of what Libby told us was bull."

She leaned over his shoulder. "What do you have there?"

"What's the difference between witches and Wiccans?" He pushed his laptop toward her.

As she leaned in closer to the screen, her hair feathered against his cheek and her perfume emanated from the pulse beating in her throat. If he didn't already know she applied a dab or two of the musky scent every morning, he'd swear it was her original smell, something organic to Christina.

"I have no idea what the difference is." She flicked the monitor. "Try this website. It looks like a directory of witches or something."

"Witchweb dot com? Catchy." He clicked on the link and a screen popped up filled with symbols and signs and links to products. "Whoa, we could spend all day on this website."

She jabbed her finger at the display. "We may not have to. There's our symbol."

"And it links to something." He brought up the next page, which contained a brief description of the symbol.

Running his finger beneath the words, he read aloud. "This symbol first appeared in the Caribbean and has been a part of Santeria practices, but today it is most commonly associated with the brujos of Mexico, especially the coven *Los Brujos de Invierno.*"

"I've never heard that name before—winter witches." She dropped to her knees beside his chair. "But Dad comes from Mexico, so it totally makes sense that he'd belong to that coven. Why would someone want to wipe out members of a coven?"

"Money? Love? Power?"

"Does it look like these people care about power or money to you?" She waved her hand at the website, and then clenched it into a fist. "Wait. The tarot card. The one with the lion and the maiden means strength. I guess that could be power."

"Power and death, right?" He tugged on his earlobe. "I was hoping there would be a directory of witches. How is the killer finding them? We need to figure that out before he gets to his next victim."

"And before we go too far down this path, we need to check the witch connection with the other two victims outside San Francisco. So far, we have the occult symbol necklace on Liz, and Nora's employment in an alternative bookstore and Libby's assurance that Nora was a member of this coven."

"Don't forget the same symbol on your windshield, which means our killer is still in the city or someone other than the killer knows about the victims' connection to this coven."

She sat on the floor beside his chair, folding her legs beneath her and tilting her head back to look up at him. "We'll have to turn over all this info to the P.D. We promised we'd share, and maybe they have something for us."

"I'd feel a lot better if my brother was in town."

"When is he coming back from his extended vacation?"

"Not until September. He's with a teacher he met on his last case."

"Your brother is actually serious enough about someone to travel with her? A teacher?"

"I know, a kindergarten teacher. I was kinda surprised, but that cold heart of his had to melt sometime."

"Well, I'm glad it was a kindergarten teacher who did the melting and not some red-hot stripper."

He laughed and ruffled her hair. "The date he brought to our engagement dinner was *not* a stripper."

"Uh, she worked at The Boom Boom Room at the edge of North Beach, and her name was Candy."

"Candy was an exotic dancer."

"If an exotic dancer takes her clothes off, she's a stripper, especially if her name is Candy."

Eric pushed away from the table and grabbed a bottle of water from the mini fridge. "Sean dated those types of women because he was always afraid of getting too close to someone. He could keep his distance with them without hurting anyone's feelings."

"Looks like he's gotten through all that if he's on vacation with a kindergarten teacher."

"Exactly why I don't want to bother him with this case." As he stepped through the door to his own room, he called over his shoulder, "I'm getting those files."

When he returned to her room, she was huddled over the laptop, her fingers racing over the keyboard.

"Find anything else?"

"Just doing some name searches, but there aren't any websites that seem to have a list of coven members."

He dropped the files on the desk. "They probably want to keep a low profile."

Someone knocked on Christina's door. "Expecting someone?"

"No, unless that's Darius Cole with more news about

Vivi." She untangled her legs and jumped to her feet. Placing a hand against the door, she put her eyeball up to the peephole and swore.

"Who is it?"

She whispered, "No one. We can just pretend we're not here."

With his brow furrowed, Eric stalked toward the door.

She slapped her hand over the peephole at the same time a voice came from the hallway.

"C'mon, Christina. It's Ray Lopez. I know you're in there, and I want this story."

Chapter Nine

She ground her teeth together and took a quick look at Eric's stormy face. He may have come to realize she was never working with Ray on a book about his family, but it didn't mean he liked the man. And she didn't need Ray complicating this tentative truce she had with her ex-fiancé and the father of her child.

Shaking her head, she mouthed, *ignore him.*

Eric reached across her and pushed down on the door handle. "By all means, let's hear what the scrappy boy reporter Ray Lopez has to say on the matter."

Eric flung open the door, and Ray jumped back into the hallway.

Ray's mouth spread into a smile. "Now I know it's a big case with a Brody in the mix. How the hell are you, Brody?"

Eric grunted in response and ignored Ray's outstretched hand.

"What are you doing here, Ray?" She wedged her hands on her hips, hoping to show her extreme displeasure at her childhood friend's appearance.

As usual, nothing got through his thick skull. He rubbed his hands together and slipped into the room. "What am I ever doing? I'm after a story. Two murders in the city and nothing from the SFPD. You know, if your brother was here, Brody, he'd give me the goods. He always gives me something."

Eric folded his arms and leaned against the doorjamb, still keeping the door wide-open. Just in case he wanted to throw Ray out?

"I guess I forgot to tell him you were ferreting around trying to get the dirt on our family."

Ray stroked his goatee. "Just the truth, man. It's still a fascinating story after all these years. I'm not the only one looking for a new angle on the story. There's a reporter up in Seattle who just hit the bestseller lists with one true crime book, and she has her eye on the Joey Brody story for her second."

Christina grabbed Ray's arm. "I'm sure you didn't track me down to discuss the ancient Brody case."

"I tracked you down because I heard you were working these two murders—Nora Sterling and Liz Fielding."

"I am." She took a step toward Eric still glowering by the door. "We are."

"That's a little," he remarked as his gaze darted toward Eric, "awkward."

Eric pushed out a noisy breath of air. "We're all adults here, Lopez. Have you heard anything on the street about the murders?"

"I'll show you mine if you show me yours first."

Christina jabbed her finger into Ray's ribs.

He gasped. "Metaphorically speaking, of course. I'm just wondering why two FBI agents are out here for a serial killer."

"Well, duh. We have a serial killer division." Christina tipped her chin toward Eric to close the door, and he let it slam.

"I know that, but usually you guys get involved when the murderer crosses state lines. Have there been other murders? Similar murders elsewhere?"

"I guess we're not going to see yours, Lopez, because there's no way we're giving up that information to a reporter." Eric practically spit out the last word.

"The press serves a valuable purpose, Brody." Ray folded his hands over his slightly paunchy stomach and raised his eyes to the ceiling.

"Prove it. What are you hearing on the street?"

Ray looked both ways and cupped a hand around his mouth. "That Liz and especially Nora were into some weird stuff."

Christina's pulse jumped. "Like what?"

"Voodoo, hocus-pocus stuff." He waved his hands in the air. "Séances, Ouija boards, conjuring spirits. Kinda reminds me of your old man, Christina."

Eric narrowed his eyes. "Maybe they conjured the wrong spirits."

Ray made a gun with his fingers and pointed at Eric. "Are the cops working this angle yet? Are you?"

"You know we can't reveal anything like that."

Ray jerked his thumb at Eric. "Have you explained how quid pro quo works, Christina? Hell, even your brother knows how it works."

"My brother is a homicide detective with the SFPD. He needs people like you." Eric brushed his hands together. "We don't."

"Aww, I'm all broken up. Didn't I just give you a choice morsel of info?"

"It ain't that choice, Lopez."

Ray wagged his finger. "Ahh, you just gave me a hint, Agent Brody. The cops *are* working this angle. You already know about the witchy ways of Nora and Liz."

Christina shoved her hands in her back pockets. "Is that all you came here for, Ray? To find out what we know about the murders?"

"That," he said, grabbing her by the shoulders and planting a kiss on her cheek, "and to say hello to an old friend. You look great, by the way."

"Thanks, Ray. You look good, too."

"Just remember to throw me a few scraps now and then. I'm not asking for anything confidential, but if you've got something you're going to release to the press anyway, think of me first."

Eric dug into his pocket and handed a card to Ray. "And if you hear anything, let us know."

Ray pressed the card to his heart. "We've come a long way, Brody."

Christina's brows shot up. Eric had taken this forgiveness thing to a whole new level.

Ray seemed to want to quit while he was ahead because he practically ran for the door. "Say hello to your mom for me out there in Nowhereville."

"Will do." She shut the door and turned slowly. "That went…well."

"I still don't appreciate that he was working on you to use me to get to my family's story, but I guess I understand him better."

"I know he's kind of a jackass, but he's just trying to make a name for himself."

"What does that have to do with pretending to have a relationship with you? He even hinted marriage."

"He's always had a little crush on me." She held up her fingers about an inch apart. "The two of us were over by then anyway. He's not a bad guy. He's helping his mom send his younger sister through school."

"Okay, enough of the sob story. If he can give us anything, I don't have a problem reciprocating with a little advance information."

The knots that had been twisting in her gut since the moment she saw Ray through the peephole began to loosen.

She liked this retro Eric Brody. This was the man she'd first met and fallen in love with. The man who'd existed before he'd started working child abductions.

What psychiatrist had told him *that* was a good idea? Instead of resolving the issues from his own kidnapping, the assignment had twisted his insides. And when his team had lost the child on that last case, he'd come unraveled.

How would he feel now to know he had a child of his own?

"Earth to Christina." He snapped his fingers in front of her nose. "Let's finish looking over the files from the other two cases and then get some lunch."

"As long as I can stretch out on the bed while doing it— looking at the files, I mean."

"Nobody told you to sit on the floor."

"Believe it or not, the floor is more comfortable than sitting at a desk. You're not the only one who gets tight muscles and backaches."

He reached for one of the files and tossed it onto the bed. "Stretch away. I'll go through the Juarez case."

Christina fluffed up the pillows against the headboard and sank against them. She flipped open the file on her lap and started with the lab report on the victim, Olivia Dearing.

For the next half hour, the silence of the room was broken only by the rustling of pages and a few clicks as Eric typed on the laptop.

Then Eric whistled. "Hello."

"Find something?"

"A few days before Victor Juarez was murdered he had a tattoo removed."

"Yeah? So what?" She swept the papers from her lap and rolled onto her stomach.

He held up a photo and waved it. "There's a picture of his left shoulder where the tattoo was removed. It's round."

"What are you saying? He had a tattoo of our symbol removed?"

"Maybe." He rose from his chair and tossed the photo onto the bed. "Have a look?"

She squinted at the reddened flesh on the dead man's skin. "It could've been any circular tattoo."

"Could've also been that coven symbol."

She picked up the photo, swinging it by one corner. "Anything in that report about what kind of tattoo it was?"

"Nope, but the name of the tattoo removal place is in here. I'm going to give them a call and see if they can remember what they removed from Mr. Juarez's shoulder. Did you find anything?"

"Not yet."

"There may be nothing in the file at all, but I'm willing to bet the connection has to be there." He returned to the desk and shuffled through the papers in the file. "Got it. He went to a dermatologist."

He reached for his phone, and Christina jabbed her finger in the air. "Speaker."

The phone rang on the other end and a woman answered. "Westpoint Dermatology."

"This is Agent Eric Brody with the Federal Bureau of Investigation. I'm wondering if you can help me with some information about a recent patient of yours, Victor Juarez."

The woman hissed. "The guy who was murdered last month."

"Exactly. Did the police already talk to you?"

"Yes. They called to verify that we were the ones who removed Mr. Juarez's tattoo."

"Did they ask you what kind of tattoo it was?"

"They just wanted to know if it was a gang tattoo, which it wasn't."

Eric slid a piece of hotel stationery toward him. "Do you remember what it was or do you have a record of what it was?"

"I wouldn't remember. I never saw it. I'm not even sure I was here when Mr. Juarez came in for his removal. When news of his murder hit the airwaves, another girl told me he'd been in here."

"Can I talk to the doctor who removed it, or do you have the tattoo on file?"

"Oh, yeah. We always keep a before and after picture. I can look it up for you, but not right this minute, and I'll also need some verification from you that you're really from the FBI."

"Understood. I'll give you the number for the FBI, my ID number and also my email address so you can email me the picture of the tattoo when you get it."

"That'll work."

Eric rattled off the information and ended the call. "I think we're onto something."

"I can't find anything on this victim that points to witchcraft." Christina shoved the case file off her lap.

"It's there somewhere." He clasped the back of his neck, tilting his head from side to side. "I need a break. Lunch?"

"Let's get out of here. It's almost worse than working in an office. It's so claustrophobic and there are no coworkers to make fun of."

"Remind me never to turn my back on you in the office."

Her phone buzzed and one glance at it caused a rush of adrenaline to course through her body. "Ah, this is a private call."

His brows shot to his hairline. Then he backed up toward his room. "Go ahead. I'm going to make a few calls myself."

He shut the door behind him with a decisive click, and she let out a breath and collapsed against the fluffed-up pillows. "Hi, Mom. How's everything going?"

"Kendall is doing fine, but she misses her mommy."

Christina put a hand over her heart where the hole just got bigger. "Can you put her on the phone?"

"Of course. She's helping me pack up a lunch for our picnic at the park. I'm meeting that nice, young mother down the street and her daughter. I think she's a stay-at-home mom."

Christina gritted her teeth and ignored the jab. "Great. Kendall and Serena play really well together."

"Here she is. Say hi to Mommy, Kendall."

"Hi, Mommy." Her daughter's sweet voice filled the hole in her heart with love.

"Hi, girly-girl. Are you going to play with Serena today?"

"In the sand."

"Are you going to build castles in the sandbox?"

"Princess castles."

"Those are the best kind." When she'd been a girl, she'd spent time building sand castles and then punching holes in them. Kendall clearly had not inherited her mother's tomboy ways.

Kendall went on to tell her about her lunch and the kitten next door, and a few other things Christina couldn't quite figure out, but she loved listening to her daughter chatter away anyway.

Then the words abruptly stopped and her mom got back on the phone. "Quite the chatterbox today."

"I didn't get a chance to tell her I love her. Can you put the phone back to her ear?"

After some rustling noises, Christina said, "Love you, girly-girl. See you soon."

"When *are* you coming home, Christina? Chasing serial killers around the country is no job for a woman with a young child, especially when that child doesn't have a father."

The guilt twisted her insides. Nobody could do guilt better than her mother—especially when she was right.

"He's here."

"What?"

Christina lowered her voice. "Eric. He's on the same case and he's here with me."

"Perfect. Now you can tell him he's a father."

"It's not that easy, Mom."

"It's not easy because you've been sitting on this bomb-shell for over two years."

"You know why I did that."

"Because he was mad at you?"

"It was more than that. He was in a dark place when he lost that kidnapped child, and he'd already told me he didn't want kids of his own. I had agreed to that, so when I got pregnant it would've looked like a trap after he dumped me."

"So what? If he's any kind of man, he'll get over it when you tell him he has a daughter."

"He'll hate me for keeping it from him."

"As he should. So that's why you're not telling him now? You think it's going to mess up the little kissy-face game you have going on now? You're selfish, Christina."

Anger pounded hot against her temples, and a retort burned on her lips. Then she closed her eyes and dragged in a breath through her nose. "You're right. I need to tell him. I will tell him."

"A man like Eric Brody will never walk away from his responsibilities. He may walk away from you, but never his daughter. He's not like your father."

Christina's eyes flew open. "Speaking of Dad, have you heard from him or Vivi lately?"

"Funny you should ask. Vivi was just out here."

"What? When?" Christina bunched the bedspread in her fist.

"A few weeks ago."

"Why didn't you tell me?"

"I forgot. That girl is loopy, and she has loopy friends. She had some guy with black fingernails in tow. I'm not sure she should be around Kendall without supervision."

Christina nibbled on the end of her own fingernail. Vivi must've still been traveling with Darius Cole. "Did she come to see me?"

"No, she knew you weren't here. She dropped by to see Kendall."

"Did she say where she was going?"

Her mother expelled a long-suffering sigh. "We didn't talk that much, Christina. I offered her lunch, but she said she was in a big hurry. She played with Kendall for a while and took off. She is Kendall's aunt. I'm not going to deny a family member—even a loony one."

"And I don't want you to." Vivi never would've attempted to test Kendall's supposed powers with Mom hovering nearby. "I'm just wondering if she said anything about where she was headed."

"Not to me, although the guy with the eyeliner mentioned something about the city. Is the cross-examination done now? We've got a playdate to get to."

"Have fun and give Kendall lots of kisses from me."

Christina scooted off the bed and paced by the window. Why would Vivi stop in to see Kendall on her way into hiding? San Miguel could've been on her way, but then she made a detour back to San Francisco.

Eric knocked on the door.

She laced her fingers behind her back. "Come on in."

He poked his head into the room. "Private call's over?"

The less she said about that call, the better. Tapping the phone against her chin, she said, "Where are we having lunch? I'm starving."

"How about Fisherman's Wharf?"

"Kind of touristy."

"I don't live here anymore. I'm a tourist."

"Bread bowls with clam chowder? All the tourists love those."

"You read my mind."

They took the Muni to the Wharf, and walked two blocks on streets crowded with performers and tourists and hustlers.

They ordered their food and carried their trays to a patio where they nabbed a white plastic table beneath a red umbrella and shrieking seagulls.

Christina dipped her spoon into the thick white chowder and stirred. "I've been craving one of these ever since I got into the city."

"I'm surprised you don't live here anymore." He broke off a piece of bread from the bowl and swirled it in the soup.

"I like the slower pace of San Miguel."

Chewing slowly, he gazed past her toward the water. "Are you seeing someone?"

"Seeing someone?" Her spoon paused in midair.

His eyes shifted to her face and locked on to hers. "Dating someone. Do you have a boyfriend?"

"Oh, God, no." Who had time to date between work and Kendall?

He raised one eyebrow and she mentally kicked herself for being so vehement.

"I just thought," he hedged as he plunged his spoon into his bowl, "the private phone call might've meant a boyfriend."

"Oh, that?" She patted her lips with a napkin. "That was my mother."

"Oh. Didn't mean to pry."

She dropped her napkin back in her lap. "You're not. In fact, she told me something strange."

"It's your mother. Strange doesn't surprise me."

"This time it wasn't how to organize my underwear drawer, although that could be coming next."

"What'd she say?"

Christina traced her finger around the soggy rim of her bread bowl. "She told me Vivi stopped by a few weeks ago."

"Really? Was she looking for you?"

"Yeah, she was." She had to come up with some good reason for Vivi's visit other than to see her niece.

"I thought that Darius character said they were in the city, and Vivi must've known where you were staying since she told Darius."

"It could've been the same time I was in Portland."

"Why didn't she just call you? She does have your number, right? Or she could've gotten it from your mom."

She held up her hands. "As far as I know she has it. But logic and Vivi don't belong in the same sentence."

"That must've been just about the same time she left Santa Cruz."

"On her way from there to here to somewhere else, but where?"

"My brother hasn't called me back either, so no progress on that front." Eric picked up his phone. "Wait a minute."

"Is it Judd?"

"An email from the dermatology clinic." He tapped his phone and whistled. "I think we just found our connection."

Chapter Ten

"Let me see. Is it the same symbol?" She stretched out her hand, but he ignored it and walked his chair next to hers.

He held out his phone with one hand, cupping it with the other. "See for yourself. Looks like Victor Juarez was a member of the same coven as Nora and Liz."

"And my sister."

"Whom we can't find."

Christina took a long pull of ice water to soothe her dry throat. "There's still Libby. Do you want to pay her another visit today?"

"I think that's a good idea." He held up another piece of bread. "Just as soon as I devour my chowder and the bowl it came in."

When they finished their lunch, they took another bus up to The Haight.

"I'm glad I'm not driving today. It's more crowded than it was last night."

"Tourists. The name Haight-Ashbury district still carries the old mystique for some, doesn't it? Even though hipsters have replaced the flower children."

"It wasn't all peace and love back then either. Don't forget Charlie Manson hung out here and hooked up with some of his disciples on these very streets."

"You would know that. Why were you reading about serial killers instead of playing with Barbie dolls?"

"Can't tell you that, Eric. I tried to explain it to you before, but I can't even explain it to myself."

"Except that you have some kind of connection with them—the killers."

"To their evil side. I wish I didn't, but there it is. Maybe it led me to this work, and it's my way of doing good. My way of taking something dark and exposing it to the light."

"I'm glad it brought you…here."

She raised her eyes to his face, but he'd turned away and was pointing ahead.

"Alley's right there. Let's see if Libby's open for business."

They turned down the alley lined with shops, which looked a little tawdry without the colored lights glowing in the dark. Libby's bookshop was situated near the Lower Haight where the Victorians were a little shabbier and the street people a little grittier. The door to Kindred Spirits was closed, but the open sign faced the street so they pushed through to the shop. The bells overhead jingled and a cloud of incense wafted out the door.

Libby looked up from her conversation with a customer and waved.

"This is the book to get you started. If you have any kind of gift at all, you'll find out soon enough when you start working with the cards."

"Thank you. I've always wanted to learn how to read tarot cards."

As Libby turned to ring up the sale, she winked at Christina.

After Libby ushered her patron out the door, she glided back behind the counter. "You're back. You must have more evidence to back up my claim."

"Maybe." Eric picked up an orb and held the blue glass to his face. "What's this?"

"It wards off evil spirits, Agent Brody." She twisted her gray braid around her hand and studied the end. "Are you in need of something like that?"

"I'm not, but members of a particular coven might be."

Christina clicked her fingernails on the glass counter. "What's going on, Libby? Why would one coven want to get rid of another?"

"I'm somewhat of a coven historian. I have traced the familial lines of the great families and have worked on the family trees, but your theory is as good as mine. I have no idea why this purge is going on."

"Has it happened before between covens?" Eric placed the glass ball back in the basket.

"Not in modern times. Not that I'm aware of."

Christina asked, "What were the reasons in the past for these types of…purges?"

Libby held up her thin hand, the blue veins crisscrossing beneath her flesh, and ticked off her fingers with each word. "Power, money, love, revenge. All the usual reasons. I'm sure you've seen it all in your line of work, and it's no different in the world of the occult."

Eric brushed her ear with a whisper. "Told you so."

"You haven't heard anything else about the murders? Did Nora ever talk to you about any of it or any of her fears?" Christina couldn't help but make comparisons between Nora and Vivi, but Vivi had known enough to go into hiding.

"I just know there was trouble brewing, but I don't know the details. I have certain…sensitivities, but I'm not a witch."

"What about Nigel?" Eric made a turn around the shop and stopped in front of a cork bulletin board.

Libby chuckled. "Nigel's an old hippie who lives on the fringes of the occult world—definitely not a witch."

"What's this?" Eric reached up and yanked a piece of paper from the bulletin board. He slapped it down on the counter in front of Libby.

She smoothed the paper with her wrinkled hands. "It looks like a gathering of witches, doesn't it? Right in the Lower Haight at the old union hall. Some say that's sacred ground for witches and brujos, a place of great power."

Christina grabbed the notice by the corner and tugged it across the counter. "What coven is this?"

"It's all covens, Christina. The individual covens are too small and spread apart to have exclusive meetings. This is a geographic coven for northern California."

"The meeting is tonight." Eric tapped the paper. "And we're going."

Libby stepped back. "You can't. They're not going to allow just anyone to waltz into their meeting."

"But I'm not just anyone." Christina spread her arms wide. "You said it yourself. People don't choose covens—they're born into them. I belong at that meeting and I'm going."

"*We're* going." Eric swept the notice from the counter, folded it and shoved it into his front pocket.

Libby's mouth hung open, her faded blue eyes wide. "You can't just barge in there asking questions like the FBI."

"We're not going to barge into the meeting." Christina clapped her hands, her heart racing. "I know the symbol of my coven, and I'm going to wear it proudly."

"Now I know you're crazy." Libby gripped the edge of the counter and leaned forward. "You'll be putting yourself in danger."

"I'll be putting myself in a position to get some information. Besides, I'll have my weapon on me."

"A gathering of witches and Wiccan is not going to let you walk in there with a gun."

"Then I'll have something better than my weapon." She jerked her thumb toward Eric. "I'll have him."

"I don't know, Christina. I'm with Libby on this one. You're going to be putting yourself in the direct line of fire. Let me handle this."

"They're not going to let you into the meeting by yourself, Eric. Besides, what do you think I'm on this job for? We're a team."

"I know that." He rubbed his hand across his mouth. "How are you going to get a necklace like the one Liz had? SFPD is not going to allow you to take that out of the evidence lockup."

"Who needs a necklace? I'm going to get a tattoo."

"That's a little extreme, even for you."

Libby shook her head. "I don't like this."

Christina rolled her eyes. "A *temporary* tattoo. With that baby, I'll have carte blanche into any witches' meeting in the Western Hemisphere."

"Tattoo parlor?"

And just like that, Eric was on board. She knew she could count on him. He definitely had that protective streak—all the Brody brothers had it—but he liked his women strong, as long as he could be there to back them up. Weak women reminded him of his drug-addled mother.

"I give up." Libby hugged herself. "Turn right out of the alley, walk a few blocks and you'll be in the middle of a whole street teeming with them. I've heard Ink Masters does good work."

"Ink Masters, it is." Eric rapped on the counter with his knuckles. "Thanks, Libby."

As they walked out the door, she called after them. "Be careful."

But the tinkling of the bells and the drumming of Christina's heart drowned out her words of warning.

Eric took her hand and laced his fingers through hers. "Are you sure you're up for this?"

"It's not a *real* tattoo, silly."

He squeezed her hand. "You know damn well that's not what I meant."

"It's just a witches' meeting. What could possibly go wrong? It's not like they're going to be practicing any human sacrifice."

"And you know this, how?"

Laughing, she dug her nails into his skin. "I think this is going to give us some good leads."

"I think you're a little too excited about being with your own kind."

She snorted and tugged on his arm. "Look. We just entered the tattoo mecca."

They strolled past a few shops until they reached the end of the block, where Ink Masters reigned supreme in the bottom floor of a pink Victorian.

"Are you sure you don't want to do this with me, for real? You know, his and hers." She tapped his denim-clad backside and it felt as good as ever.

He turned a dark green gaze on her, hot enough to melt her little gold earrings. "Only if I can pick the precise spot on your body."

Prickles of heat needled several precise spots on her body. "Umm, just kidding."

He opened the door for her and as she brushed past him, his whispered words followed her into the tattoo parlor. "I wasn't."

She turned sharply, but he was studying the tattoo

designs on the walls with an impassive face. Had she imagined those words?

A young woman, a sleeve of colorful art creeping down one arm, stepped from behind the counter. "Can I help you?"

Christina swallowed, looking at the woman's impressive ink and hoped her request wouldn't get her laughed out of the shop.

She cleared her throat. "I'd like to get a temporary tattoo. Do you even do those here?"

"Absolutely. Saves you from getting it removed later when," she whispered, her eyes flicked to Eric as her pierced nostrils flared, "you dump the dude."

"Oh, it's not for, uh, a dude. There's a symbol I'd like you to re-create for me."

Eric pulled the dog-eared piece of paper from his pocket and shook it out. "Can you duplicate this?"

The woman shrugged a pair of skinny shoulders. "Piece of cake. Just tell us where you want it."

"And the color?" Suarez's tattoo had been black and red.

"We use a henna tattoo, so it'll be a reddish-brown color." She wrinkled her nose. "We don't use the black henna. That stuff's vile."

"I'll take your word for it, and I want the design on the inside of my wrist." Christina rotated her arm to reveal her inner forearm.

"Let me have the pattern, and I'll give it to J.C. He does most of our henna temp tats since he has a light touch."

After several minutes, J.C. emerged from the back, heavily inked, like all the tattoo artists in the place. He led her to a reclining chair and cleaned her skin and his hands. "This is an interesting design. What is it?"

"It's a Wiccan symbol." She watched J.C.'s face closely for any kind of reaction, but he didn't blink an eye.

"Are you a Wiccan? I know a couple of Wiccan, but between you and me I think they're BS-ing me."

"It's all in fun, really." She settled against the chair and closed her eyes while J.C. started working on her arm.

Eric chatted with J.C. about the tattoo artist's process and some of his weirder requests.

In less time than she thought possible, J.C. was putting the finishing touches on her temporary tattoo. "Let me know if you want any changes."

She inspected her new ink. "Looks just like Victor's, doesn't it?"

"Except the colors." Eric lightly clasped her wrist and held her arm up to the light.

"Lilith explained about the henna, right? Can't do different colors."

"Oh, yeah. She told us. No problem."

"If you like it, you can come back for the real thing and you can have any color you like." J.C. gathered his tools and went off to his next canvas of flesh.

"I like it. What do you think?"

"If it helps us get into the meeting tonight, I'm all for it." Eric pulled out some cash to pay for the tattoo and ducked his head to place his lips close to her ear. "Somehow I don't think the Bureau would appreciate reimbursing us for a tattoo."

"I don't know why not. It's a work-related expense."

"I'll let you explain that to Rich."

As they strolled back onto the street, Christina held up her arm to admire her new ink. "I kind of like it."

"Maybe you shouldn't flash that around." Eric took a step in front of her as if to shield her from unwelcome attention.

She poked him in the back. "That's the point, isn't it?"

"For tonight, but you don't have to bring any weirdos out of the woodwork before the meeting."

"Maybe you're right." She pressed her arm against her side. "I'd like to get back to the hotel and give that case file another go. Now that we've definitely linked Juarez to the other two victims, I'm positive we'll find something on the very first victim to tie her to all of this."

"Maybe Olivia kept a lower profile—no tattoos, no jewelry, no working in occult bookstores."

"Her killer identified her somehow. There must've been something she did or had that marked her as a member of this coven." She fished some bills out of her pocket as the bus squealed to a stop at the curb. "I'll get your bus fare."

They hopped on the bus, and a young man sporting an Afro with a silver streak jumped to his feet and waved her to his seat.

She thanked him and settled in the seat, while Eric hung on to the handrail above her. When the bus bolted into traffic, Eric's hips jerked dangerously close to her face.

She let her gaze linger on the way his abs tensed beneath the soft cotton of his T-shirt and how the denim hugged his muscled thighs. Excitement bubbled through her blood at the thought of working with him tonight. The hint of danger only heightened the thrill. That's how they'd fallen in love in the first place.

When he'd broken off their engagement and left her, he believed she'd sought him out because he was Joseph Brody's son and she'd been enthralled by the story of a homicide detective turned suspected serial killer. And he was right.

But once she met Eric Brody in the flesh, his father's story couldn't compare to the powerful connection she'd felt for him right from the start. The connection they felt for each other.

She felt it again. It never left. She had to try to make him understand her reasons for keeping the pregnancy from him, but her mother was right. Even if the truth turned him from her once again, he'd never turn from his daughter. He had a right to know his daughter.

"This is us." He tapped her on the head, and she grasped the bar to pull herself up.

The bus lurched to a stop, and she swayed against him, her breasts brushing his chest.

"Whoa." He curled an arm around her waist to keep her there, and his heart pounded against her chest.

Was the beat faster than normal? Harder than normal? Did he feel the connection again, too?

They jumped onto the sidewalk seconds before the bus rumbled forward.

Eric coughed as the exhaust rolled over them. "We seem to be having some major problems with vehicles in this city."

"Do you think the car last night could've been an accident?"

"After someone left you that symbol on your windshield?" He brushed two fingers across her new tattoo. "Seems like a big coincidence."

"Could've happened to any pedestrian on a crowded street."

"But it happened to you."

"Then maybe I didn't even need the tattoo." She stabbed the button for the crosswalk signal. "Maybe I'm already a marked woman."

They sailed through the hotel lobby and stepped into the elevator with another couple and a flushed-faced businessman who kept glancing at the floor numbers. All three of them got off on the same floor, and when the doors shut, Eric crowded her into a corner of the car and placed his hands against the wall on either side of her head.

"Promise me you'll be careful tonight."

She painted a cross above her heart with the tip of her finger. "I promise."

She'd promise him anything right about now if he'd stay right where he was. No, maybe a little closer.

He did a push-up off the wall and retreated to his side of the car. "Sorry. I just know how intense you are and how much you get caught up in your work. Worries the hell out of me."

She blinked, trying to shake off the spell his hazel eyes cast on her.

"Nobody's going to try anything at the meeting, especially with a roomful of potential mind readers."

The doors slid open on their floor, and all the pent-up emotion between them seemed to flow out into the hallway and dissipate.

Eric paused at his door, his card hovering above the slot. "The meeting's not until ten. Maybe we should order room service and relax."

"I'm going to relax with that file and see if I can find the connection for Olivia."

"Don't work too hard. I'm going to start putting together a report for Rich and the SFPD."

They both slipped into their rooms, and Christina slumped against the door. Relax? How could she possibly relax when the man she'd been yearning for was right next door, within her reach for the first time in two years?

Within her reach but separated by a gulf called Kendall Rose.

Chapter Eleven

Eric fired up his laptop and printed out the picture of Juarez's tattoo—just like Christina's. How had he let her talk him into that?

His rational side replied correctly that it wasn't his call to make. Christina was his equal partner. She was an FBI agent and a damned good one. She might be soft and pliable in bed, but that's not where he had her…yet.

He plowed his fingers through his hair and growled low in his throat. Wasn't it just a matter of time? He knew it and she knew it.

His eyes strayed to the connecting door. Maybe he should barge right in there and get it over with.

Dragging in a ragged breath he pulled out the desk chair and plopped down in it. Work. He needed to get this stuff down in a report to his boss. The SFPD would appreciate a heads-up, too, and would expect it of Detective Sean Brody's brother.

He opened a file and started typing, the blank screen filling up with black words keeping his mind off the woman next door.

He worked for another hour, transferring information from his scribbled notes and random pieces of paper to the orderly file taking shape before him.

He pushed back from the desk and stretched at the same

moment his phone buzzed beside the laptop. He lunged for the phone and saw his brother's name on the display.

"Where the hell have you been?"

"Don't hate on me, but I've been working in Maui."

"Good for you, Judd. Glad to see you gainfully employed."

"Yeah, I've been bodyguarding that little actress from that new werewolf TV series."

"Okay, I'm officially hating on you."

"But I've got good news for you."

"You found Christina's sister?"

"Are you back with Christina? It's about time, bro."

"I'm back working with her, and you didn't answer my question."

"Vivi Sandoval is in Mexico."

"How'd you discover that?"

"I'm a P.I.—I never reveal my sources, unlike you loose-lipped fibbies."

"Is she okay?" Eric stretched out on the bed.

"Yeah. Shacking up with some older dude. Is she missing or something? She's a little old to be running away from home."

"Christina was worried about her. Vivi doesn't have her phone."

"I didn't think the two of them were that close."

"She's the only sibling Christina has."

"Unlike us lucky SOBs, right? If you're in the city, have you seen Sean?"

"He's on an extended vacation right now—with some teacher."

"Yeah, yeah. I heard something about that." Judd cleared his throat. "You need anything else? Because right now the actress is getting ready for a private luau—you know, piña coladas, hula girls, warm Hawaiian nights."

Eric snorted. "Don't work too hard…bro."

He closed his eyes and crossed his arms behind his head. At least he had some good news for Christina. She'd mentioned her father was in Mexico, so Vivi was probably with him—the powerful brujo.

The rap on the door jerked him out of dreamland and he rolled from the bed. Rubbing his eyes, he opened the door to Christina's room.

She jabbed a finger in the air. "You've been sleeping."

"I kind of dozed off." He yawned. "But that report's going to be in good shape for Rich on Monday morning."

"I had no luck at all with Olivia." She flicked her fingers in the air.

He grabbed her hand, sporting new black nail polish. "I see you've been hard at work at the salon downstairs."

"Oh, these?" She curled her fingers and inspected her fingernails. "Thought I'd better get a little more in character."

"Do you really think witches wear black nail polish?"

"Vivi does—and lots of black eyeliner, and let's not forget Darius."

"Which brings me to my next piece of news. Judd called. Vivi's down in Mexico, probably with your dad."

She squealed and threw her arms, black nail polish and all, around his neck. "That's awesome news. Judd is the best. She's okay?"

"As far as his source could tell him, she's fine. If she's with your dad, he'll protect her, right?" Since her arms were still around his neck, his curled naturally around her waist.

"Absolutely. There aren't many in the occult world who are going to mess with Octavio Sandoval."

He kissed her forehead because, well, his lips were so close anyway. "Good. At least that's one issue we can put to bed—to rest."

"Are you hungry?"

Her plump lips were close, too, and he *was* hungry, hungry for her touch. "I'm starving, and there's nothing dampening my appetite now. No barriers between me and the feast before me."

Her body stiffened in his arms, and she placed her hands flat against his chest. "Except maybe work."

He dropped his arms. "Work."

"Do you want to show me that report?" She twirled away from him.

It took him several seconds to catch his breath and dial back on the lust that had surged through his body parts. Either he'd been misreading her signals or she'd just gotten cold feet.

Or maybe it's because she'd gotten the information she needed about Vivi out of him.

"Report, yeah." He strode to the laptop and woke it up. The neat report with its bullets and columns and pictures flashed on the screen. "Knock yourself out. I'm going to look at the room service menu."

The words on the plastic menu blurred before his eyes. What kind of game was she playing with him? Why was nothing ever as it seemed with Christina?

"Great job, partner."

Okay, she'd just officially put him back in the friend zone. "Thanks, partner. Maybe I should give Olivia's file the once-over. You could be missing something because you're too close to this case now."

"Maybe." She wedged her hip against the desk, keeping her distance. "What looks good on the menu?"

"Depends. Do you want something like a sandwich or a real meal?"

"If we're going to be fighting off witches tonight, I'll take the meal. Steak? Potatoes?"

He waved the menu in the air. "They have both. Salad, too."

"The works."

He ordered the food to be delivered to her room. Seemed safer over there.

By the time the cart arrived, he'd gained control of his senses and his libido. He needed to keep his distance and his sanity.

He'd ordered the stuffed pork chops and garlic mashed potatoes. Lots of garlic—a remedy for both vampires and romance.

"How's your steak?"

"Good. How's your chop?"

He stabbed a piece of meat. "Great. Is pork really white meat, and does that mean it won't go with this red wine?"

She cupped the half bottle of wine in her hand and read the label. "It's a cab. It goes with anything."

"Your impressive wine knowledge is really coming in handy." He waved his hand across her body. "What are you wearing tonight, a black hat and robe?"

"You're very funny, Brody." She swirled her wine in her glass. "I'm sure witches come in all shapes and sizes and walks of life. Look at the killer's victims."

"We should at least try to blend in, and that means black, just like your nails."

"I can manage that, can you?"

He tossed his napkin onto the tray. "Absolutely. Ever since Judd got me into motorcycles, I've been adding more and more black to my wardrobe. It's hard to ride a bike in beige khaki."

"The next time you talk to Judd, thank him for me. I feel a lot better knowing my sister is probably with my dad, although I wish one or the other of them would've called me."

"Is your dad in the habit of calling you?"

"No."

"Does he favor Vivi?"

"Of course. She took up the family line of work, but she

needs him more than I do. Her own mother died when she was a teenager."

"Was her mother a bruja, too?"

"No, just another groupie."

Eric held up the bottle of wine. "Do you want the rest?"

"As long as we're not driving."

She held out her glass and he rose from his chair and poured. "How come you never told me all the details about your family before? I never realized their powers went so deep."

"I wanted to marry you, not send you screaming for the hills."

"And my background with a suspected serial killer for a father is so much better?"

"That doesn't reflect on you."

"Neither does your family." He gathered his silverware and dumped it onto his plate. "I think if you had told me, it would've helped me understand where you were coming from regarding your interest in serial killers. Maybe I wouldn't have gotten so upset about the notes."

"Yeah, you would've. It was a bad time for you, Eric. I just wish..." She crossed her own fork and knife on the edge of her plate and glanced up brightly, blinking her eyes. "I wish you would've stuck around longer to give me a chance to explain everything."

She didn't trust him not to run out on her again. Is that why she was holding back? He'd had his trust issues. It never occurred to him until this second that she had her own with him. He'd ended their engagement and had escaped to parts unknown—unknown to her. He'd made sure she had no way to reach him.

He had to be alone to grieve the loss of Noah Beckett and his own urges to recover what was taken from him as the result of his own kidnapping. If he had been able to bring home every kidnapped child to their parents, he believed he could've filled that hole in his soul. But he'd failed.

He had given himself a big mountain to climb and he'd slipped off the edge.

"Do you want to give me that file before I retreat to my own room?"

"Oh, are you leaving? You don't need to. We still have a few hours before we have to get going. I was just going to kick back and watch some TV—unless you don't think you can concentrate on the file with distractions."

He scratched his chin. She was the biggest distraction of all, but if she wanted him to stay he would. "I always work with background noise. Mind if I camp out on the love seat?"

"Be my guest, and don't you dare shave."

"Huh?" The plate he'd been stacking on the tray clattered as he dropped it.

"The stubble works—black shirt, stubble," she said with a grin as she flashed him a thumbs-up, "you're in with the brujos."

He shook his head and hoisted the tray. "Just don't expect me to cast any spells."

Her luscious lips curved into a smile. "I couldn't imagine that, but the scruff should stay."

He opened the door and propped it open with his foot as he placed the tray on the carpet outside. "I'll keep it. Now let me have a crack at that file."

"It's on the bed."

He sat on the edge of the mattress and reached across the rumpled bedcovers to grab the file folder. Christina's scent engulfed him and he almost burrowed into the covers to get lost in it.

He gripped the edge of the folder and resurfaced to reality. "I'll give this a fresh set of eyes."

She dropped to the bed just as he cleared it, punched

some pillows into place and settled against them. She aimed the remote at the flat screen TV. "I'll try to keep the sound down."

"Believe me, I'll let you know if it's too loud." He sprawled in the corner of the love seat and dropped the folder in his lap.

Once he got engrossed in the details of the case, the TV really did become background noise. Even Christina's presence faded to one corner of his mind.

After about an hour, he tilted his head back against the cushion and closed his eyes. As his muscles relaxed, the sounds and smells of the room came back into focus. Once again Christina's perfume tickled his nose, and the droning voice on the TV began to form actual words.

He listened for several minutes and then opened one eye. "Are you watching a true crime show?"

"It's about that murder up in Seattle, the father who killed his family and tried to blame it on intruders."

"Yeah, that guy's a straight-up sociopath—dead eyes."

"Remember when Ray was telling us about that reporter-turned-true-crime-writer who wrote a book on this case?"

"Yeah, the one who's interested in my father's case?"

She pointed at the TV. "There she is. They interviewed her as part of this show."

He dropped his chin to his chest and squinted at the screen. An animated brunette was waving her hands around, punctuating her words with gestures. "Okay, remind me never to talk to her."

"She's fascinating. She interviewed the guy in prison, and he turned on the charm thinking he'd get favorable treatment in her book. Guess she saw right through that because her portrayal of him is not at all flattering."

"As a sociopath, he probably thought he had her wrapped around his finger."

She muted the sound. "I probably should've been watching that dancing show or something."

"You don't have to hide your interests from me, Christina. I already know you're kind of morbid."

"Speaking of which, it's time to get into character."

"I'll leave you to get ready. I'm going to try to catch a few winks before we go."

"I'm too wound up to nap. I'm going to hop in the shower. I'll knock when I'm ready."

"And the file?" He tapped the folder. "I didn't find anything either."

He retreated to his room and spread out on the bed, setting the alarm on his phone for a wake-up call in forty-five minutes.

It came all too soon. He took a quick shower and pulled on some black jeans, black T-shirt sporting an old album cover from The Who and a pair of motorcycle boots. Just as he stomped the second boot on the floor, Christina tapped on the door.

He called out, "I'm ready."

She peeked around the edge of the door and whistled. "You look hot."

"For a brujo."

"For anything." She widened the door and stepped through, her black skirt rustling around her ankles.

"And you look appropriately witchy."

She'd outlined her eyes with black liner and tousled her dark hair so that it hung like a disheveled curtain around her shoulders.

Rotating her arm outward, she said, "The tattoo is the perfect touch, don't you agree?"

"Looks like it belongs there permanently." He took her untattooed arm. "It's showtime."

They took a taxi to The Lower Haight where the crowds were thinner, the Victorians shabbier and the transients more aggressive. They had the driver drop them off up the street from the meeting address, and Eric kept feeling for his nonexistent weapon. He felt naked without it, but he didn't want to risk getting kicked out of the coven's meeting for packing heat.

They reached the location of the meeting, a run-down union hall, which didn't much look like sacred ground. An unofficial welcoming committee greeted them at the door.

A middle-aged woman, who looked nothing like a witch in her mom jeans and cardigan, eked out a tight smile. "Newcomers?"

As soon as they walked through the doors, Christina's knees weakened and trembled, and her heart started racing. Her feet felt rooted to the floor.

Eric shot her a curious glance, and then draped his arm around her shoulders, pulling her flush against him. "We're visiting from New Mexico and saw the meeting notice at Kindred Spirits. Is this a West Coast meeting?"

The woman's eyes darted toward her companion, a young man with small sharp teeth. Now *he* could be a witch.

He pulled a white handkerchief out of his sleeve and dabbed his nose. "Bay Area coven."

Christina reached up to pull her hair back from her face, flashing her tattooed wrist. "We like to check in with other covens when we travel."

The effect of the tattoo was immediate. Both sets of eyes glommed on to the symbol, following the movement of Christina's hand.

"You made it." A familiar voice called from across the room and Nigel, dressed all in black for the occasion, limped across the floor, his hand outstretched.

Eric shook his hand and squeezed it hard. If Nigel blabbed about the FBI, it would be all over.

"Do you know them, Nigel?" The woman narrowed her eyes, still focused on Christina's tattoo.

"I met them in Libby's place. We had a chat, and this young lady's the real deal, unlike yours truly."

Eric finally released the older man's bony hand. "Like I said, we saw the meeting notice at Libby's and decided to check out the meeting. I hope that's okay. We haven't had any problems anywhere else."

The man with the bat teeth nodded. "No problem, hombre."

As they walked across the floor to a table laden with refreshments, Eric murmured, "For a minute there I thought you were going to blow our cover."

Nigel put his finger to his lips and studied the plates of cookies before choosing an oatmeal raisin. "I may have screamed 'down with the pigs' in my younger days, Brody, but sometimes authority is a force for good."

"Only sometimes?" Christina picked up a chunky brown cookie and sniffed it. "Are you sure nothing here is laced with anything?"

Nigel stretched his thin lips into a grin. "Didn't you notice the fruit punch? There are no mind-altering drugs, including alcohol, allowed at the meetings. That cookie you're holding may have some kind of grass cooked into it, but not the kind you're thinking."

She broke the cookie in half and large crumbs dropped to the table. "This definitely is not my thing. I'm going to grab one of those brownies with the cream cheese frosting on top. Do you want the healthy vegan cookie, Eric?"

"No, thanks. You touched it, broke it apart and sniffed it. You'd better not put it back on the plate."

"Ha, that's something that Ken…" She dropped the cookie on the floor and bent over to sweep it up with a napkin. "That's something a kid would do."

Eric pointed to the black smudges that stained a huge area of the scuffed floor. "This building ever catch on fire?"

Nigel stirred sugar into his coffee. "This union hall was built on hallowed ground. At the height of the flower power movement here in the Haight-Ashbury district, witches would come to this building to cast spells and work powerful magic with incantations and ceremonies."

Christina shivered. Maybe that's why she'd felt the air being sucked out of her lungs when she'd walked through those doors.

The woman who had been guarding the entrance tapped on the microphone at the front of the room. "We're going to get started in a few minutes. If you haven't partaken of the refreshments, please do so. They're all home-baked by our Bay Area members."

Christina crumpled the napkin with the broken cookie in it and whispered to Eric, "Doesn't mean they're good."

The woman's announcement caused a surge for the refreshments, and Eric took Christina's arm and led her to a folding chair in the back row. They took the seats on the end of the row, and Nigel sat in front of them.

"Do you know what to expect?"

Christina shook her head, her wild hair cascading around her face. "I have no idea. I doubt if my father or Vivi ever attended anything like this."

"Do you think they'll talk about the murders?"

"I can't imagine they know much. If they had an idea members of a particular coven were being targeted, don't you think they would've gone to the police?"

He swiveled his head around. "This bunch? I'm guessing they have an innate distrust of authority, and wouldn't be too anxious to hold themselves up to ridicule."

"Maybe you're right." She tapped his thigh. "Let's listen."

After forty-five minutes of mind-numbing bylaws and

politics, Christina jabbed Eric in the side with her elbow and rolled her eyes. "This is boring. When does the spell casting start?"

"I think this may be all they do. Uh-oh." He jerked his head forward and to the right. "Isn't that Darius Cole, Vivi's friend? If he sees us, he might rat us out."

She slumped in her chair and peered between some heads and shoulders. "I can't tell if it's him or not. I'll make sure to stay out of his way as I grab another one of those brownies. I have to keep awake somehow."

At that moment the Witch of the West made an announcement. "We'll take a fifteen-minute break. Bathrooms are available and there are plenty of refreshments and hot coffee."

Christina jumped from her hard seat and squeezed past Eric's knees. "You see, she does read minds."

She shuffled up to the table and ducked between two men to grab her brownie.

"Those are yummy, aren't they?"

She turned with her mouth full to face the speaker. Chewing, she pointed to her mouth and made noises. She swallowed and licked the sweet frosting from her lips. "Sorry. Yes, those are the best. Did you make them?"

"Goodness, no. I bring the coffee." The young woman's gaze had strayed to Christina's tattoo. She tilted up her chin. "You belong to that coven from down south, the one with its roots in Latin America."

"You know what they say." Christina traced the henna tattoo with her fingertip. "You don't pick the coven, the coven picks you."

"For some it works that way, but a lot of people are just posers." She sliced her arm through the air, taking in half the hall.

"Are you?" Christina offered her hand. "I'm Christina, by the way."

The woman took her hand in a limp grip. "I'm Uma, and I wouldn't say I'm a poser, but I'm not the real deal. Are you the real deal?"

"Yes." Christina raised her chin. "It's in my blood."

Uma looked to the left and then her right before taking a few steps closer to Christina and invading her personal space with her musky scent. "That might not be a good thing to brag about right now."

Christina's heart thumped so hard, she feared it would cause the chains around her neck to jingle. "Because of those murders?"

Pressing three fingertips against her lips, Uma nodded, her light-colored eyes wide.

"Who is it? Who's going after my coven?"

Uma dropped her hand and raised her voice. "I'm going to beat you to that last brownie."

Christina jerked her head up to find that several groups of people had clustered around the table, chatting in low voices. Had she and Uma been overhead? Did it matter?

If this was a real meeting of the Bay Area covens, they should be talking openly about the threat—unless the threat was here, under this roof.

All of a sudden, the sweetness of the cream cheese frosting soured in her mouth and she reached for a foam cup and filled it with black coffee. She'd need it to stay awake. Who knew witches could be so boring?

She slurped a few sips of the hot beverage as the clutches of people began to break up. Some had heard enough and headed for the exits, while others ambled back to their seats.

Uma ducked in front of her and tossed a napkin into the trash. "If you're drinking coffee, you'd better hit the bathroom before Elaine starts up again. She frowns upon people walking out on her."

"Just as long as she doesn't turn me into a frog." Christina smiled and raised her cup.

Uma didn't appreciate her attempt at humor and frowned. "The bathrooms are out back, across the quad."

"Thanks."

Christina glanced back at Eric and Nigel still talking. At least she had something to report to Eric. Uma knew about the murders and had tied them to the coven—and was afraid to talk about it openly. Maybe Uma would join her in the restroom and give her the rest of the scoop away from finely tuned ears.

Grasping her cup with two hands, Christina wandered toward the back doors of the room. The wind tossed her hair when she stepped outside. She grabbed her skirt with one hand to keep it from billowing around her. Tilting her head back, she caught a glimpse of clouds scudding across the dark sky.

She crossed the empty quad, veering to the left.

The building across the quad ended in a blue door with no label and a weak light spilling over it. Christina tried the handle, but it wouldn't budge.

Maybe Uma just wanted her outside to meet with her in private.

"Uma?" The wind snatched her voice and carried it away.

She peeked around the corner of the building and saw another door. Crossing her arms and dipping her head against the wind that whipped around the corner, she headed for this second door.

She grasped the handle and it turned, so she yanked open the door. The breeze skittered behind her, blowing dry leaves.

Dry leaves in the middle of the summer? She half turned and a dark shape barreled toward her out of the shadows.

Chapter Twelve

An arm slammed her face-first into the metal door. Her tongue smashed against the chipped paint. The coffee sloshed over the rim of the cup and scalded her hand.

Strong fingers gripped the back of her neck and squeezed so hard she couldn't drag in a breath.

She'd caught a glimpse of a black mask before the attack, a black mask with eyes cut out. Glittering eyes.

Her hand still stung from the coffee as it dangled at her side. The smell of formaldehyde burned her nostrils, and a surge of adrenaline coursed through her veins.

"Christina?"

Eric's voice echoed from across the quad. The pungent odor of the formaldehyde grew stronger. Eric might not reach her in time.

With a burst of sheer will, she jerked up her arm and tossed the coffee into her attacker's face.

He grunted and stumbled back.

She slipped from his clutches and clung to the side of the building, scrambling for the corner. She screamed Eric's name but it came out a whimper.

She flung herself into the quad, falling to her knees.

"Christina!"

Eric dropped beside her and she bunched his shirt in her fists and rasped, "Go get him...around the corner."

"Are you all right?"

"Get him."

He pulled her against the wall of the building and propped her up. Then he took off around the corner.

The door to the bathroom banged open, and Eric shouted something unintelligible.

Had he found him? Christina held her breath.

Then she heard footsteps and the rattling of a chain-link fence. "I think he went over the fence."

She braced her hand against the rough, uneven wall and pushed herself up. She edged around the corner.

Eric stood at the end of the cement walkway, clinging to a chain-link fence and shaking it.

"I-is he gone?"

"Looks like it." He strode back to her and engulfed her in his arms. "What the hell happened out here? I thought you went for a brownie?"

"I had to use the restroom, and someone attacked me from behind. Pinched my neck and was about to douse me with formaldehyde. He was distracted by your voice and I threw coffee in his face."

His arms tightened around her. "Christina, that's not a restroom."

"What are you talking about? Uma told me they were out here."

"Who's Uma?"

"A woman I met by the brownies—tall, blond curly hair. She told me the ladies' room was across the quad."

"There's a unisex bathroom right by the hall entrance. That's some utility room."

"Oh, my God." She put a shaky hand to her forehead. "Uma, she lured me out here because she knew someone was waiting for me."

"I'm sick of this secrecy." He cinched an arm around her waist and started crossing the quad.

She dug her heels into the cement. "Hold on. What are you doing?"

"It just became open mic night at this boring meeting, and I'm taking the floor."

"Eric, I'm not sure this is a good idea."

"Sure it is. Are we going to cower outside and pretend you weren't just attacked?"

He pushed through the door back into the hall, and marched to the front of the room, his motorcycle boots clomping on the floor.

"What are you doing? It's not time for question-and-answer yet."

"Sure it is, Elaine." He grabbed the microphone from its stand on the podium and crossed in front of the room.

"My partner here was just attacked outside in the quad. A woman named Uma sent her out there looking for the restroom."

Murmurs rose around the room and furtive glances were exchanged.

"Yeah, I said partner. She and I are with the FBI's serial killer unit and we're investigating the murders of Liz Fielding and Nora Sterling, and two other murders of a man and a woman out of state."

It seemed as if everyone let out their breath at once or let loose some giant hissing snake.

"We know the murders are connected to a particular cult, *Los Brujos de Invierno* and we want some answers."

The chanting started in the back of the room, and goose bumps spread across Christina's flesh as more and more people took up the chant.

"Simbala, sarai, simabala, sarai."

It swirled around the room and Christina had to grab the back of a chair to stay upright as the sibilant sounds washed over her.

Eric was gripping the microphone with two hands,

a scowl creasing his face. His eyes sought hers, but she shrugged weakly.

When the chanting had subsided to a whisper, Elaine stepped toward Eric and asked for the microphone.

"We're sorry your partner was attacked, Agent Brody, but that's what happens when you play with fire."

"What are you talking about? What was that chanting?"

"The coven you speak of has turned to the shadows. The members of that coven have always flirted with the dark side. You of all people should understand that."

"What? How would I know that? I don't know anything about this coven except that some of its members have a bull's-eye on their backs."

"And we're sorry for that, too. We knew Nora. She didn't practice the dark arts, but it's guilt by association."

Eric pressed the heels of his hands against his temples, probably to keep his head from exploding. "Are you trying to tell me that some other coven or some witches are eliminating members of this coven because they're evil? Sort of an internal housecleaning?"

Elaine spoke into the microphone. "This meeting is over. Please clean up after yourselves, and someone put the trash out."

Eric crossed his arms and rested one booted foot on a chair. "Are you going to answer me?"

"Why? You've figured it out."

"But who is it? I don't care what the motivation is, it's still murder and you said yourself, Nora didn't deserve to die."

She lifted a shoulder. "We don't know who it is."

"And if you did, you wouldn't tell us anyway."

Her other shoulder joined its mate, and then she crouched down to unplug the mic.

"Wait a minute. How did you know my name?"

She twisted her head to the side and met his eyes with hers. "I'm a San Francisco native. I know the Brody story."

A finger poked his gut, sending a quiver of unease up his spine. What was it with these witches and his family? What did the suspicions about his father have to do with a coven of witches?

"You can't condone what's happening now to innocent people."

"We don't condone it, but we're powerless to stop it."

Christina asked, "What was that chanting for?"

"To ward off evil at the mention of that coven."

"You're confused. I think the person who's doing the killing is the real evil."

"If you knew what that coven was capable of, you wouldn't be sporting that tattoo. If you know what's good for you, get it removed."

The lights flickered once and the hall cleared out.

Before she locked the door, Elaine turned to them. "Are you going to call the police?"

Eric leaned against the wall where Christina stood hugging herself. He should be the one doing that. "Do you want to report your attack to the police, Christina?"

"No. They're not going to find anything, and I don't want them smirking behind my back."

"It wouldn't do any good anyway." Elaine hitched a huge bag over her shoulder and ambled down the sidewalk.

He trailed his fingers down the angry red marks on Christina's throat. "Are you sure you're okay?"

"Do you think he was going to kill me?"

"With a little formaldehyde? I doubt it."

"A warning, then? He couldn't have thought he could drag my limp body over that fence."

Eric smacked his hand against the closed door of the union hall. "This little charade raised more questions than it answered, didn't it?"

"We know the motive now."

"Is that really the motive? Who knows?"

They walked down one block to a busier part of the district, and Eric pulled his phone from his pocket. "I'm going to call a taxi."

She rubbed his arm. "I'm okay. Are you? All these people seem to know you."

He ordered a taxi and shoved the phone back into his pocket. "I don't understand why all these old witches seem to know Brody business. What was it about my father's case that attracted their interest? You should know. You're an expert on my father's case."

Biting her lip, she kicked the curb with the pointed toe of her shoe. "You said it yourself. One of your kidnappers was wearing the same necklace that Liz Fielding had on at the time of her death—the symbol of the coven—the dark coven, apparently."

A taxi barreled down the street and did a U-turn, pulling to a stop in front of them. They collapsed in the backseat and Eric called out the name of their hotel in Union Square.

"Where was Nigel after the break?"

"He left."

Christina sucked in a breath. "Before or after my... encounter in the quad?"

"Before." He took her hand and toyed with her fingers. "He's pretty old. Do you really think it could've been him?"

"Maybe the stiff posture is all an act."

"I doubt it. Would help if we could locate Uma. She's the one who told you to go out back."

"What about the guy you thought was Darius?"

"Never got a good look at him. I think he left at the break, too."

"I don't think any of those people necessarily want to help. It's like they're giving their tacit approval of the decimation of this coven." Her gaze slid to the back of the driver's head, but the radio and the street noise from his open window kept him oblivious to their conversation.

"Why would they want innocent people hurt? Unless…" He rubbed the scruff on his chin with his knuckles. "…they're not so innocent."

"By all accounts, Nora was a sweet girl."

"All accounts or just Libby's? Nora worked for her. Do you think Nora would discuss her penchant for black magic with her employer?"

"What about Liz Fielding?"

"It's in the report—junkie, former prostitute, petty thief."

"So, that makes her a devil worshipper?"

"No, but she was no saint either." Keeping possession of Christina's hands, he turned to face her. "That meeting didn't give us what we expected, but it did give us something. Someone thinks this coven is on the wrong track, and that someone has taken matters into his own hands."

Her hand wriggled from his grasp, and she pounded her chest with her palm. "But what about me? Why go after me?"

"You came in wearing the symbol of your coven proudly." He traced the circle with his nail. "What were they supposed to think?"

"So the person who attacked me may not even be the killer or in with the killer. But why the formaldehyde? Were they expecting us?"

The taxi shot across the tracks ahead of an oncoming cable car and squealed to a stop in front of their hotel.

Eric paid the driver and grasped Christina by the shoulders before they went inside the hotel. "I don't know if they were expecting us or not. I don't know if the symbol on your car windshield and the near miss in the crosswalk were threats to you or warnings. But I think we need to dig a little deeper into the victims' lives—not what they showed the public, but what they were doing behind closed doors."

When they got to their rooms, Eric followed Christina into hers.

Eric wore a path from the window to the door, his hands clasped behind his neck. "What do you think this coven's involved in?"

Christina stretched out on the bed and toed off her shoes which fell to the floor with one clump and then another. "I don't know."

She patted the bedspread beside. "You look so tense. Sit down."

He paused in midstride, dropping his arms to his sides. "I guess there's nothing we can do about anything right now. I'll add tonight's festivities to my report. The cops are going to want to know why you didn't report the attack."

"Maybe we shouldn't tell them." She waved him over. "Let me work some of those knots out of your shoulders, and if you don't mind, snag one of those bottles of wine from the minibar for me."

He crouched down in front of the minibar and selected a little bottle of white wine from the door. "Is this okay?"

"I don't care what it is. I just need something to take the edge off. Those people at the meeting alternated between boring and creepy. I'm so glad I didn't sign up for that craziness."

"Did you ever have the opportunity?" He twisted the lid from the bottle and picked up a plastic cup. "I thought your mom put the brakes on that when you were a toddler."

"She did, but that didn't stop Dad from checking in occasionally to see if I wanted training."

"Training?" He poured the wine for her and handed her the cup. Then he sat on the very edge of the bed.

"According to my father, we come from a long line of very powerful brujos. He thought I was wasting my heritage."

"You have to be trained?"

"Oh, sure, it's like anything. The latent power or talent may be there, but if you don't know how to develop it you'll never reach your potential."

"Sort of like a school for witches?"

"More like homeschooling." She sipped the wine and closed her eyes as the warmth spread throughout her limbs. "Let's give it a rest—for now."

She placed her cup on the nightstand and rubbed her hands together to warm them up. Skimming her fingers along the base of his neck, she asked, "Do you want me to give it a try?"

His broad shoulders rolled forward. "Sure."

She dug her fingers into his warm flesh and kneaded. "Feel good?"

"Feels great, but you're the one who was slammed into a building tonight."

"My nerves are still a bit jumpy, but the wine will help with that." She dug the heel of her hand into the top of his shoulder. "And don't worry because I don't make a habit out of self-medicating."

"I'm not worried. I can't imagine you being addicted to anything."

Except you.

Wasn't the definition of addiction having a compulsion for something you knew was bad for you, but indulging anyway? That summed up how she was feeling right now.

She knew Eric wanted her again. He said it with his touch, with his eyes, with his willingness to join her on the bed.

But he wouldn't be here if he knew the truth. Was it so wrong for her to enjoy one night with him before reality came crashing down around both of them?

"Ouch!"

"I'm sorry. Did I hurt you?"

"It hurt so much, it felt good." He let out a long breath.

"I don't know how you have so much power in those long, thin fingers of yours."

Leaning over his shoulder, she flexed her fingers. "It's magic."

He caught her wrists and pulled her onto his lap.

She widened her eyes. "How am I going to massage your back from here?"

"I have other body parts that are more in need of a massage." He quirked his eyebrows up and down.

She snorted. "Where did you learn that line?"

"You mean, it didn't work?"

"Did I," she said as she straddled his thighs and draped her arms around his neck, "say that?"

He put his hands around her waist, pulling her closer. "I always was a smooth one with the lines."

The kiss he planted on her lips had the effect of ten glasses of wine as warmth flooded her body. She leaned into him, deepening the kiss, exploring his mouth with her tongue.

It felt as if the two years they'd been apart had never happened. The taste of his mouth, the pressure of his thumbs on her rib cage, the way his beard scratched her chin—the feelings rushed back in, overwhelming her.

He fell onto his back, whether from the enthusiasm of her embrace or his own desire to position her body on top of his, she didn't know or care.

Their legs dangled off the edge of the bed while their torsos met along every line. His hands swept beneath her blouse, spanning her bare back. He unhooked her bra, and then his fingers crept toward the waistband of her skirt. He felt for the zipper and slid it down.

He rose to his elbows beneath her. "Can we stretch out on the bed so I don't lose circulation in my legs?"

She rolled from his body into the stack of pillows crunched

against the headboard. "I don't want you losing circulation anywhere."

Chuckling, he sat up and pulled off his motorcycle boots. Then he pulled his black T-shirt over his head and threw it over his shoulder.

She crossed her arms behind her head and smacked her lips.

"What am I, a piece of meat?"

Her eyes roamed over his bare torso and zeroed in on the bulge in his tight jeans. "Mmm, yeah."

He grabbed her legs still hanging off the edge of the bed, and swung them around so that she was stretched out on top of the bedspread. Her skirt gaped open where he'd unzipped it before, and he pulled it over her hips and down her legs.

She kicked it off. "Never liked that skirt anyway."

"I like it—off." He ran his fingertip along the top band of her black thigh-high stockings. "These are kind of kinky."

"I can leave them in place if they turn you on."

"This," he murmured as he rolled one stocking down over her thigh and calf and then pulled it off, "turns me on."

He gave the other stocking the same treatment. The bed dipped as he straddled her hips and fumbled with the buttons of her blouse.

"You'd better take over before I pop these buttons."

She crossed her hands over her chest. "Now this blouse I like."

She unbuttoned each of the tiny pearl buttons until the blouse fell open. He'd already unhooked her bra and it lay across her breasts, barely covering them. She hoisted up to her elbows and shrugged out of the blouse and bra. She swept them off the bed with one impatient motion.

His hands took the place of her bra as he cupped her breasts, running his thumbs across her peaked nipples.

She watched him out of half-closed eyes, breathing in

his scent. She'd never forgotten it. When he left her, he'd left a T-shirt behind in her laundry basket and she hadn't washed that T-shirt for months. Slept in it even as her belly grew bigger with Kendall.

She squeezed her eyes shut. *Don't think about the lie right now. Don't think at all.*

He buried his face between her breasts and kissed the insides. "Some women have all the luck, don't they?"

"Like me? I *am* enjoying myself, but you've gotten a little cocky, haven't you?"

He swirled his tongue around one nipple, and she gasped.

"I meant," he said, touching his tongue to the tip of the other breast, "you've put on a little weight since I last saw you, but it went to all the right places. I've always loved your breasts, but now they're lovable and luscious."

"I never realized you were such a breast man."

"I wasn't—not until the precise moment I saw yours."

To emphasize his point, or maybe just to drive her crazy, he sealed his mouth over her right breast and suckled her.

Her hips jerked up, and she moaned. "I think my younger, smaller breasts feel jealous."

He murmured something since he obviously didn't want to release her. And she could totally live with that.

She reached for the belt on his jeans. "Why do you even still have these on?"

"Protection." He laid a kiss on her mouth. "Did you always talk this much during sex?"

"You're the one analyzing my body parts." She yanked on the buttons of his fly and thrust her hand into the gap. "Did any of your body parts get bigger in the past two years?"

"Yeah, baby. Just you wait and see."

"I know your lines have gotten cornier." She peeled his jeans from his narrow hips and tugged on his briefs. His erection filled her hand.

She widened her eyes. "Oh, yes, much bigger than I remember."

"You don't have to be sarcastic about it." He staggered from the bed and pulled off his jeans and briefs, letting them drop to the floor. "One last item."

Hunching forward, he grabbed the waistband of her panties and yanked them down and off her body.

She squirmed and reached out to him, wiggling her fingers. "You can't just leave a girl naked without warming her up."

He fell on top of her heavily, and she accepted the weight of him, welcomed it.

She wrapped her legs and arms around him as if to keep him in place.

He showered kisses on her face. "I was such an idiot. I should've been doing this twenty-three months ago. Stupid pride."

She didn't want to talk, didn't want to think. Threading her fingers through his thick, wavy hair, she lifted her head to kiss his mouth. He sealed his body to hers even more, his erection probing her thigh.

He growled in her ear. "Are you ready for me?"

The ability to speak had escaped her, so she just nodded.

"Let me see."

He inched down her body, leaving a trail of kisses and nibbles and then thrust his tongue inside her.

Gasping, she cradled his head with her thighs. And then the teasing began. He sucked her into his mouth, driving her to the edge of madness. Pulling back, he tested her with his fingers and she closed around him with a moan.

His tongue circled her heated flesh again and she pumped her hips in encouragement. This time when his lips drew her into his mouth, she exploded.

While her climax rocked her body, he drove into her,

extending the exquisite pleasure that engulfed her. As their hips joined together, moved in unison, he buried his face into her neck.

As his lips pressed against her throat, she could feel his bared teeth against her skin. She whispered, "Let go."

His body stiffened and then he plowed into her deeper and deeper, crying out his release, and she took all of him. She'd always take all of him.

When her cell phone rang, it took her several seconds to recall where she was. Hell, it took her several seconds to recall *who* she was.

Then the adrenaline pumped through her body. The phone.

Eric growled, his voice muffled between her breasts. "It's after midnight. Who's calling you this late?"

"I—I…" His body was still crushing hers and she couldn't move, couldn't breathe, couldn't get to her phone.

He reached it first, and the lighted display illuminated the scowl on his face. "Oh, my God. It's your mother. And I was ready to go another round with you."

Christina huffed out choppy breaths. *Kendall.* It had to be Kendall.

"Give it to me." Her voice grated against her own ears, and Eric's eyebrows shot up to the tousled lock of hair hanging across his forehead.

He handed the phone to her, and shifted off her body.

With trembling fingers, she tapped the phone to answer it. "Mom? What is it?"

It must've been the quaver in her voice that made Eric's head jerk up. Now he'd be listening to every word she said, and she couldn't ask him to leave—not now.

Her mother's voice soothed on the other end. "I'm sorry to call you so late, but Kendall had a nightmare. You know—one of *those* nightmares."

"I-is she okay now?"

"She's shaky. I got her to stop crying, but only because I promised to call Mommy. She needs to hear your voice, Christina."

"Of course. Put her on."

"Mama."

"Hi, girly-girl. It was just a dream."

"I was scared, Mama. Where are you?"

"I know they're scary, but they're just dreams. They can't hurt you."

She could feel Eric's eyes burning a hole in the side of her face.

"Sleep with Mama."

"You can sleep with G-Ma. I'll be home soon." She made kissing noises into the phone. "I'm sending smooches to you."

"Got them."

Her mom came back on the phone. "She's okay. She just needed to hear your voice. She'll probably forget about it tomorrow."

"Was it the same nightmare?"

"Same thing—people standing around chanting. Oh, she doesn't call it chanting, but that's what it sounds like to me."

Christina shivered. She'd heard enough chanting for one night.

"Let Kendall sleep with you, Mom."

"I will, just like I did when you had nightmares."

Christina didn't want to end the call and face Eric, but she didn't have a choice. She cupped the dead phone between two hands and stared down at it.

Eric's low voice sounded a million miles away. "What was that all about? Who's Kendall?"

"Kendall's my daughter." He sucked in a quick breath, and she looked up finally to meet the green flame in his eyes. "And yours."

Chapter Thirteen

The sledgehammer hit him between the eyes and he blinked. The room tilted. He opened his mouth and closed it again.

Christina's chest rose and fell, her eyes never leaving his, never flinching. Clear and full of truth for the first time since he saw her here.

"How old?" He smacked his forehead with the heel of his hand. "She's gotta be, what, two? Two and a half?"

"Kendall's two."

He clenched his jaw so hard it ached. "I was right about you in the first place, wasn't I? You're a liar, a deceiver."

Her dark eyes filled with tears, which rapidly rolled down her face. "You have to let me explain."

"Why?" He dragged a hand through his hair. "Why is it you're always explaining yourself to me?"

"Just let me…"

"It's late. I'm tired." He scooped up his clothes from the floor and stalked to the adjoining door. He slammed it because it gave him something to do and made him feel better. Then he clicked the dead bolt, which made him feel even better.

He dropped his clothes on the floor and fell across the bed. He had a daughter, a two-year-old daughter named Kendall.

And Christina had kept her from him.

The next morning he studied his face in the mirror above the bathroom vanity. He didn't look any different. He didn't look like a father.

A million questions assailed his brain, and he didn't want to speak to the one person who had all the answers. How long had she planned to keep him in the dark? Until Kendall was eighteen?

Kendall. Kendall Brody. He liked it. Unless it was Kendall Sandoval—he liked that, too.

He stepped into the shower and let the hot spray pummel his back. He still had Christina on his hands and lips. He turned to face the showerhead, grabbing the little bar of soap from the shower caddy. He lathered up his hands and washed away her scent, opened his mouth and filled it with water.

Who was he kidding? He'd never wash her away. And if he wanted to be a part of his daughter's life, he'd have to find some way to work with Christina. He did want to be a part of Kendall's life.

Even though he'd never wanted kids. He'd made that clear to Christina before they'd gotten engaged. She was fine with it—then.

Is that why she hadn't told him about her pregnancy?

He cursed and aimed the spray of water at his face. Why was he making excuses for her? She'd gotten pregnant and had a baby, his baby, and never told him about it. How did you excuse that?

He finished his shower and got dressed. Standing in the middle of the floor, he stared at the door leading to Christina's room. What now? They still had a case to solve.

His gaze shifted to his laptop on the table by the window. And he had a report to finish for Rich and the SFPD. Hell, maybe the SFPD could take over from here. They'd know the local witch scene better than he and Christina did.

Although she seemed to know more about her father's

coven than she'd let on—just another deception on her part. She was probably holding out on him so she could swoop in and solve the case by herself.

He twirled the chair around and straddled it, resting his chin on the back and skimming the words of his report.

He reached around the chair, brought up a search engine and typed in Kendall Brody. Did a two-year-old have an internet footprint yet? A Realtor and a weathercaster popped up. He tried Kendall Sandoval next and found a collegiate volleyball player. What did he expect to find? All of the answers lay on the other side of that wall.

The knock came and he closed out of the search engine. "Yeah?"

"Can we talk now, Eric? If you don't want to, I understand."

He slid off the back of the chair and threw the door open. She'd replaced her high heels with flip-flops and her shorter stature made her look vulnerable and small. Probably calculated.

"Come on in." He turned his back on her and retreated to the window. He tugged on the rod for the filmy white curtains and gazed into the bustling street below.

She remained standing, too, twisting her fingers in front of her. "I want to tell you why I kept Kendall from you— at first—because I always planned to tell you about her."

"When you needed help with college expenses?"

She pressed her lips together. "Before that. I'm not gonna make excuses for myself, but we had decided we weren't going to have kids, right?"

He nodded.

"You had some crazy idea that you wouldn't be a good father because of your kidnapping experience, or maybe you were just afraid. I could never fathom the big strong Eric Brody being afraid of anything, but I saw what happened when you lost that kid."

"Noah Beckett." His shoulders ached with a heaviness he thought he'd shrugged off a year ago.

"I remember his name." Her words were a whisper. "Noah's death only convinced me further to keep my pregnancy from you. I know you blamed yourself for that debacle, but it was the Bureau, the Bureau's policies, not you that caused Noah's death."

"When did you know you were pregnant?" His jaw felt stiff as he formed the words.

"I suspected just about the time the Beckett case ended."

"That's a pretty way of putting it."

She flicked her fingers in the air. "Then I knew for sure after you discovered my notes, accused me of using you to write about your family and then dumping me. I found out for sure then."

"And you didn't get on the phone and let me know, why?"

She laughed, a hard and brittle sound. "Hello, Eric? You had just dumped me because you didn't trust me, and now I was pregnant when I'd already agreed to your no-kids policy. Yeah, that would've gone over really well."

"So? At that point, it was no longer about you."

A shaky breath escaped her lips and she dipped her head, her long hair falling across her face. "I realize that. There was also the small matter of contacting you. You'd taken a leave of absence, dropped off the radar. Nobody knew where you were. Your brothers didn't know, or you'd given them orders not to tell me."

A ball of heat lodged in his chest. His loyal brothers.

"I returned. I returned to the Bureau."

"You call working in South America on an undercover drug task force returning? I was supposed to drop that bombshell on you under those circumstances?"

"You have an answer for everything, Christina. You always did."

Closing her eyes, she dragged a breath through her nose, her nostrils flaring. "Do you want to know about your daughter? See her pictures?"

"Of course."

"Now you want a child because you have one?"

"Give me a break."

Color flooded her cheeks, but she pulled her phone from her back pocket. "I have just about every stage of her life on my phone."

"Then, thank God for cell phones."

She perched on the end of the love seat. "D-do you want to join me?"

He took two long steps toward the love seat and sat on the cushion next to her. His weight made the sofa dip, and she tipped toward him, brushing his shoulder. He stiffened and she pulled away.

Holding the phone in front of him, she said, "First pics are from the hospital."

The phone display came alive with a picture of Christina, her hair scooped back in a ponytail, smiling into the tiny face of a baby—his daughter.

He took the phone from her and held it up to his face, drinking in the little button nose and the wide eyes below a tuft of dark hair peeking from a pink cap.

He breathed out one word as his throat tightened. *"Beautiful."*

"Her name's Kendall Rose Brody."

He twisted his head to the side. "Same middle name as my mother."

"I know that." She leaned over and swept her fingertip across the display. "Next."

His little girl's life flashed before him on the cell phone display. It was like time-lapse photography, watching her change from newborn to chubby-cheeked baby to a mobile creature crawling and scooting on the floor. She resembled her mother, but he could see his features in her. The pictures and Christina's constant commentary filled him with longing…and resentment.

After she showed him the last picture, a dainty toddler in head-to-toe pink, hugging a stuffed white bear, he collapsed against the back of the love seat.

"She's sweet and wonderful, and I want you to meet her as soon as we wrap up this case—if you want to."

"Of course I want to see my own daughter. Whatever gave you the idea that I wouldn't want to know my daughter? What gave you the right to keep her from me?"

She sighed. "I'm sorry, Eric."

He closed his eyes, blocking out his daughter's face and the years of memories he'd lost. "I was working on the report for Rich. I'll email it to him tomorrow morning."

"Sounds good. I'd like to talk to Nigel today if we can find him."

Back to business. "Do you still think he attacked you last night?"

"No, but he might know who Uma is, and since he seems a little less connected to the whole coven thing, he might be more forthcoming about what this coven has done that's so bad and who'd want to take them out."

"It just so happens," he stated as he pushed up from the love seat and shuffled through the file on the desk, "I got his card last night."

"Really?" She pocketed her phone and joined him at the table. "What does an old hippie do for a living?"

He flicked the card between his fingers. "He restores old books."

"Interesting. I wonder if that's what brought him into Libby's shop in the first place."

"Most likely. I'm going to get some breakfast and work on the report. I'll give Nigel a call."

On the one hand, he wanted Christina to ask to join

him so he could grill her some more about Kendall, but sitting across from her would be hard. Before that phone call last night, they'd given in to the sexual heat that had been simmering between them for the past two days. The sex had been mind-blowing, and he'd been ready to take her again—before the phone call.

Her phone rang and she answered it, putting it on speaker. She didn't have a need for any more private conversations.

"Hi, Mom. How's Kendall this morning?" Her eyes met his as she talked on the phone.

"She's good. I told you she wouldn't remember much."

She paused and held up her finger to him. "I told Eric about Kendall."

That was obviously for his benefit, but it did make it more real.

"He's eager to meet her, and yeah, he's pissed off at me." She raised her brows at him.

Was that to verify that he was eager to meet Kendall or that he was still pissed off at her? Right on both counts. He nodded.

"After this case. I'll see if he wants to come down to San Miguel."

She ended the call and faced him with her hands on her hips. "Do you want to?"

"Do I want to what?" He swung the chair around and tapped the keyboard of the laptop.

"Don't pretend you weren't listening to every word we were saying."

"Guilty." He threw up his hands.

"Do you want to come with me to San Miguel when this case is over to meet Kendall?"

"Of course. What does she know about me?"

"She just knows her daddy is busy working." She bit her lip.

Maybe it was better if she didn't sit across from him at the breakfast table.

"I'm gonna head out for some breakfast."

"Okay. I'm going to grab a bagel from the coffee place downstairs, hit the hotel gym and take another crack at that case." She turned at the adjoining door. "Let me know what happens with Nigel, okay?"

"Will do."

She closed the door and kicked a stray shoe across the room. He wanted to get as far away from her as possible. But she didn't blame him.

The Kendall slide show went over well, but it must've twisted the knife a little to see all that he'd missed.

It had all seemed so clear-cut two years ago. Now looking into Eric's face, she didn't know what she'd been thinking. Okay, so she'd ruined any chance she had of reconciling with him, but he seemed excited about meeting his daughter. Maybe he'd forgive her by the time Kendall got married.

She picked up the room and the evidence of a night of passion that had taken a wrong turn—actually had been derailed. Hell, it crashed and burned. But not before Eric Brody had satisfied every need she had and some she didn't even know she had.

She headed downstairs to the lobby, keeping an eye out for Eric—just in case he changed his mind about breakfast.

She bought a banana and a bagel and perched on a stool at one of the high tables scattered around the coffee shop.

As she spread cream cheese on one half of the bagel, her phone rang. Was Eric lonely? She grabbed the phone, but the display showed a blocked number. She answered anyway.

"Christina, it's Vivi."

Christina's pulse jumped. "Vivi, are you still in Mexico?"

Her sister clicked her tongue. "How did you know that?"

"I had someone track you down. I was worried about you after your friend, Darius, found me and told me you were missing."

"Darius contacted you?"

"He was worried. Why didn't you tell him where you were going?"

"I don't trust anyone right now and neither should you. How did you track me down? Who found me?"

"My coworker's brother. He's a private investigator. Don't worry. He's not going to tell anyone where you are. What's going on?"

"I was in danger, Christina. I'm fine now, but you're not."

"If you're talking about this purge of Dad's coven, I know all about the danger."

"How do you know about any of this? You've never been involved before."

"I'm working a case, Vivi."

"Isn't that a…coincidence?"

She knew Vivi didn't believe in coincidences. "Yeah, it is. I work murder cases, Vivi."

"Just be careful, Christina, and don't believe everything you hear."

"What is that supposed to mean?"

"It means there's no reason for our coven to be targeted. There are always a few bad apples that taint the rest of us. There's something else going on."

Christina sucked a smudge of cream cheese from her finger. "What exactly have these bad apples been doing?"

Her sister whispered, "Black magic."

Despite the tourists trooping through the brightly lit lobby and the customers lining up at the coffee shop counter, Christina felt a cold line of fear creep up her spine.

"What does that even mean, Vivi?"

"I'm not going to get you involved any further than you already are."

"I am involved and if it helps me solve this case…"

"It won't. You won't. And the people on the other end of this thing? They're not as appalled at the coven's actions as they'd like everyone to believe."

"What are you saying, Vivi? Help me out here."

"Let someone else handle this case, Christina. Get off it. You're exactly who they want."

"Stop talking in riddles and give me some names." The pause on the other end of the line went on for several beats. "Vivi? Vivi?"

She smacked her phone on the table. Why had her sister even bothered to call? She didn't need a warning. She needed answers.

She finished her breakfast, tossed her trash in the garbage and then headed for the gym. She may not find the answers she needed on the treadmill, but at least she could work off some of this stress.

She returned to her room an hour later and sat down with the report. The words began to blur together. *Come on, Olivia, where's the weird stuff you were into?* From all accounts, Olivia had lived and worked in Portland quietly as a waitress at an upscale restaurant—nothing strange in her background, no enemies.

Eric knocked on the inner door.

"It's unlocked." He may be keeping her locked out, but her room and her heart were wide-open to him.

He stepped into her room. "Are you hungry? We're having lunch with Nigel in Chinatown."

"Is he willing to talk?"

"He's meeting with us, which is more than anyone else will do."

"Did you tell him what happened last night after he left?"

"I figure we'll surprise him and watch his reaction."

"Speaking of surprises, Vivi called me from Mexico."

"Was she able to clear up anything?"

She swung her legs off the bed. "Just made it murkier. She knows about the vendetta against the coven, but she's not convinced it's because someone's trying to stop their evil ways."

"She admitted that the coven was involved in something evil?"

"She dismissed it as a few bad apples." She snagged her purse from the coat hook by the door. "How's the weather outside? Do I need a jacket?"

"It's warm, and we'll be walking to Chinatown." He shoved his hands in his pockets. "Did Vivi explain why someone would be after the coven if not to stop them?"

"She was full of mysteries, but she implied it was because they wanted what the coven had." She had no intention of telling Eric about Vivi's warning to her. It would come across as an appeal for his protection. Not that she didn't want or need it.

He snapped his fingers. "Power. It's why he's leaving that tarot card."

They ambled down the hallway toward the elevator. If they didn't keep talking about the case, they had nothing. She smacked the button with her palm. "Where'd you have breakfast?"

"That little outdoor café on the square. You?"

"Grabbed a banana and bagel downstairs and then went to the gym."

"Any good? The gym?"

"It was okay. Lots of free weights." She squeezed his biceps. "Are you still lifting?"

Dumb question. She'd seen his body last night in all its glory.

"When I get the chance."

They both stared at the light blink through the floors and then started talking at the same time.

"You go." She wiggled her fingers in his direction.

"I just wanted to ask if you talked to Kendall today?"

"No. Mom assured me this morning that she'd recovered from her nightmare. She's pretty talkative for a two-year-old, but they're still not great on the phone."

"Do—do you ever talk to her over the computer?"

"Yes." He wanted to see and hear his daughter. "Would you like to, I mean, do you want to sit in the next time I do?"

"If that's okay." The doors of the elevator opened and he wedged his arm against the doorjamb to keep it open for her. "I don't want to freak her out or anything. I can stay off camera."

"You wouldn't freak her out."

"Does she have these nightmares often? Sounded like it wasn't the first time."

"Every few months, but she forgets them quickly. It's funny, I used to have them, too, so my mom tells me. I don't even remember them."

"Used to have them? You were still having nightmares when I met you."

She tilted her head as the automatic doors of the hotel whisked open. "Those were dreams, not nightmares."

"They're dreams now because you made sense of them and sorted them out, but they'd be nightmares for a child."

She curled her hands into fists. "That's why I've never told Vivi about Kendall's nightmares. Vivi has this crazy notion about testing Kendall's level of perception."

"Not," he turned to her and wedged a thumb beneath her chin, saying, "going to happen."

"Oh, you don't have to tell me that. I already nixed it." Eric's parental instincts were kicking in already, and he hadn't even met Kendall yet.

They walked across Union Square and up a few blocks,

passing beneath the arch that signified the beginning of Chinatown.

Families and tourists clogged the streets, dipping in and out of shops and browsing through trinkets set out on the sidewalk.

They ducked inside the restaurant where they were meeting Nigel, and the cool darkness enveloped Christina along with scents of garlic and hot peppers.

Nigel waved a folded newspaper at them from a corner table. When they approached, he stood up and pulled out Christina's chair. "Welcome, welcome. I'll pour the tea."

As they sat, Nigel aimed a steady stream of pale green liquid into the delicate cups.

Christina inhaled the fragrant essence of jasmine, slipping into a relaxed state. She wrapped one hand around the warm cup and sipped. She skimmed a finger down the plastic menu and asked, "Are we ordering for the table? Because I'm just going to steal tastes of your food anyway."

"Table style." Nigel winked. "So tell me what happened last night. I heard all hell broke loose."

Eric finished his tea in one gulp and poured more. "Who told you that?"

"I have friends in high places."

"Did they give you the details?"

"I'm persona non grata in those circles now. They think I brought you in."

Christina closed the menu and tapped it on the table. "I was attacked. A woman named Uma sent me outside, across the quad to look for the bathrooms and I was met by a masked man with a formaldehyde-soaked cloth."

Nigel's gray brows jumped. "I didn't hear that. Are you okay? How'd you get away?"

"Eric came looking for me. My assailant got distracted by his voice and I tossed some hot coffee in his eyes."

Nigel rubbed his own eyes. "Look for someone with some burns around his eyes."

"Right, in all of San Francisco." Eric twisted his head around to look for the waiter.

"Then you crashed back into the meeting and accused everyone there of a conspiracy?"

"We asked about Uma." Christina tipped a menu toward Nigel. "I'm assuming you don't know her either since the name didn't register with you when I mentioned her."

He held up a crooked finger. "Hold on."

The waiter approached the table and took their order.

Nigel took a sip of water. "Okay. What did Uma look like?"

"Blonde, medium height. Looked about thirty."

"Attractive?"

"I'd say so. She was wearing jeans and an embroidered peasant blouse—loose and flowing."

"I think I saw her, but I didn't recognize her."

Eric asked, "Did you see her talking to anyone at the meeting?"

"Geoffrey Vandenbrook. You met him. He was at the front door greeting people, the one with the teeth filed to points."

"Was he just greeting her, or was it something more sinister?" Christina swirled the last drops of tea in her cup.

"I have no way of knowing that, Christina. You're the one with the special powers." Nigel rearranged some plates on the table to make way for the steaming dishes the waiter was rolling over on a cart.

They all kept quiet while the waiter placed the plates on the table along with bowls stuffed with mounds of white rice.

Ignoring the food, Eric picked up his fork and aimed it at Nigel. "I thought you had something to tell us, something about the coven that's being targeted."

Nigel turned one of the bowls upside down and the rice plopped onto his plate. "I do have something to tell you, Agent Brody, something about the past, not the present."

A tingle of apprehension rippled through Christina, and she crumpled the napkin in her lap.

"Spill it." Eric's shoulders lifted.

"This coven from south of the border has been involved in misusing its powers for the past twenty-five years or so. This latest spate of bad behavior is nothing new."

"The past twenty-five years?" Eric's voice sounded tight, matching his face.

"And twenty years ago, they were involved in a kidnapping."

Eric dropped his fork. "What are you trying to tell me?"

Nigel pinched a piece of chicken between his chopsticks and held it up. "I'm telling you, Agent Brody, that this coven was involved in your kidnapping twenty years ago."

Chapter Fourteen

Eric snapped his chopstick in two. How many more bomb-shells could he take this week?

"Are you sure about this?" Even as he said the words, a vision of that necklace hanging from the female kidnap-per's neck flashed in his head.

"Most of the occult community in the Bay Area knows it to be true."

Eric's gaze wandered to Christina, who crossed her chopsticks in front of her. "I'm not part of the occult world, and I certainly didn't know about it."

"I don't understand." He dumped some rice on his plate, followed by some shrimp. "My kidnapping was connected to the serial killer my father was investigating. Some said that he arranged the abduction himself to throw the police off his trail."

"Do you believe that? Did you ever believe that?"

"I didn't hear the stories until later, and I didn't know what to believe. Are you suggesting that the real serial killer contacted this coven to kidnap me, or that my father himself contacted them?"

"I don't know anything more than the fact that the coven was involved." He screwed up his lined face and chased a peanut across his plate with his chopsticks.

"This is just too incredible to believe."

"Believe it or not, it's the truth, and that's why so many in the occult world know about you and your ordeal as a child."

Again, he glanced at Christina, who had filled her plate with food.

"Stop looking at me like I'm the devil. You know I have minimal contact with my father and sister, and we certainly don't discuss coven business when we do talk."

"It's all so," he mused as he made a ball with his hands, "circular."

Nigel cocked his head. "Life is that way, isn't it? I'll leave it to the two of you to piece together, since I'm sure there are things you can't discuss in front of me."

"Let's lay this out. This coven, in which Christina's family has a prominent…"

"Wrong already." Christina tapped his water glass with her chopstick.

"Correction. This coven, to which Christina's family belongs, but is not involved with, started using its powers to perform evil deeds. The witching world let it go for a while and then some rogue witch started taking action by eliminating the members of this coven—whether or not they were involved in any of the black magic."

"Don't forget my sister's take." Christina glanced at Nigel. "She believes there's another reason someone is targeting the coven—because he or she covets their dark powers."

Nigel nodded. "Not out of the realm of possibility. Where is your sister?"

"Sealed to secrecy." She drew a line across the seam of her lips.

"That could be. I'm giving you what I know. I've always been peripheral since I don't have the gift myself. There are a lot of us like that—on the outside looking in."

"You sound…regretful." She waved a spoon over the

plate of kung pao shrimp. "Does anyone want to split the rest of this with me?"

Eric nodded. "I will."

Pushing his plate away, Nigel said, "I am regretful. I'd like to experience having the power that you choose to neglect."

"I'm not interested in abracadabraing my way through life."

"You joke about it, but isn't it clear we're dealing with some powerful forces?"

"It's clear we're dealing with a bunch of people who are putting too much stock into some extrasensory feelings. These people in my father's coven who are turning to crime, like kidnapping, are just bad people. They don't have any more power than any other criminal." She popped the last piece of shrimp in her mouth.

He shook his finger at her. "I wouldn't be so sure of that."

The waiter dropped off the bill and Nigel pushed back from the table, dropping his napkin in his plate. "I'm assuming you can write that off as a business expense, since I'm a witness or something, right?"

Eric picked up the check and waved it at him. "We've got it."

Nigel bowed, placed a gray felt fedora on his head and hobbled from the restaurant.

Eric stared after him with narrow eyes. "How far do we trust him?"

"Are you changing your mind? Do you think he might be involved in the murders?"

"I don't know." Eric reached for his wallet and snapped his credit card onto the tray. "All that stuff about members of the coven being involved in my kidnapping."

"It makes sense, Eric." She tapped her chest. "You recognized the necklace. Nigel didn't know anything about that memory."

"If it's all true, maybe the Phone Book Killer was part of the coven. If I can find out more about what went down, I can clear my father's name once and for all."

"And solve this case?"

His chest flashed with heat. "Do you think I'm losing focus?"

"I think—" she dabbed her mouth with her napkin as she spoke "—you've been careening from one shock to another."

"It seems like we're both a little too involved in this one."

"My involvement is giving me some insight and access that we might not have gotten."

"Your involvement is putting you in danger." And even though she'd been deceiving him about their daughter for the past two years, he wouldn't stand by while the threats piled up against her. Kendall needed her mother.

"It comes with the territory. Are you ready to get out of here?"

"Have you forgotten something?" He grabbed one of the fortune cookies from the tray and cracked it open. He read aloud from the slip of paper. "You are headed in the right direction. Trust your instincts."

Christina clapped her hands. "Perfect. It means we're going to solve this case."

"As long as I trust my instincts." He tossed a cookie to her. "What's yours?"

She bit into half of the cookie and pulled the fortune out of the other half. "Something special is coming your way."

"There you go. That means we're going to solve the case."

"That would be great, but if that's your fortune, I'm hoping my something special is something more personal." She dropped the slip of paper into her purse and stood up from the table without meeting his eyes.

If she was hoping they'd work things out, she was being

premature. Could he ever forgive her? Her deception raised all his issues of distrust with her. Right now he just wanted to take it step-by-step. Get through this working relationship with her and then meet his daughter.

He pushed the door open for her, and they both stepped onto the crowded sidewalk. He turned right to go back to the hotel, but she plucked at his sleeve.

"I'm not going back to the hotel just yet. I'm going to take the afternoon off and browse through Chinatown a little, and then maybe head to North Beach and get a gelato."

"Do you think that's a good idea?"

"Because someone attacked me at a meeting of the Bay Area covens? It's broad daylight."

"You're forgetting the mishap in the crosswalk."

"I'll look before I cross. Besides," she patted her handbag and whispered, "I'm armed."

He didn't like it, but she was a professional. He couldn't expect her to lock herself in her hotel room.

Shoving his hands in his pockets, he turned and called over his shoulder, "Be careful."

She stood rooted to the sidewalk, watching Eric's stiff back retreat. She could've invited him to come along, but she wanted him to make that suggestion.

Since she showed him the pictures of Kendall, it seemed as if he was always on the verge of saying something. She knew he wanted to ask her a million questions about their daughter. She'd hoped they could discuss Kendall over a couple of gelatos or cappuccinos.

Hunching her shoulders, she pivoted on the sidewalk and dodged the press of people who all seemed to be walking against her.

What forces had brought her and Eric together on this case? What forces had brought her to Eric in the first place? Her father's coven had been involved in Eric's kidnapping twenty years ago. Crazy and yet so perfect.

The baskets of trinkets lining the sidewalk drew her like a magnet, and she sifted through them. They were too small for Kendall, but she discovered a bin of small silk purses in jewel tones that Kendall would love. She could put her treasures in them or carry them as a purse.

She bought three in different colors and dropped them into her bag. She zigzagged down one of the alleys and inhaled the fresh-baked scent from the small fortune cookie factory. Maybe she should buy a fresh batch and hope for a better fortune.

Her steps took her through Little Italy, but she couldn't find the gelato shop she remembered. The gelato idea had lost its luster anyway as a solo endeavor. She continued to the edges of Little Italy where the restaurants and coffeehouses turned into bars and a few strip joints, and the tourists had thinned out.

She glanced over her shoulder. Why had someone attacked her last night? Did they really believe she was some wicked witch of the west, or was she getting too close to the truth?

Huffing out a breath, she shortened her steps as the sidewalk started climbing. She didn't feel as if they were getting close to the truth. She paused at the top of the hill to take in the view of the bay. She hadn't meant to walk this far. The streets before her crisscrossed up to Coit Tower. She definitely wasn't up for a walk uphill.

She turned to walk back the way she came—and there he was.

ERIC PAUSED BENEATH the Chinatown archway and looked back. He shouldn't have let her go off on her own, gun or no gun, pride or no pride.

He pulled out his cell phone. They had GPS trackers installed on their phones. If she was sitting at an outdoor café in North Beach enjoying a gelato, he'd be able to tell pretty quickly.

He pulled up the GPS app and tapped in Christina's number. The map popped up, and a red pinpoint located Christina's phone.

He shaded the display with his hand and swore.

She'd come out on the other side of North Beach, through the seedy part, and looked to be heading up to Coit Tower. What the hell was she doing?

Holding the phone in front of him like some sort of beacon, he made his way back through the streets of Chinatown, shouldering through the crowds. He kept glancing at the phone to make sure he was heading in the right direction.

The tourists thinned and his heart hammered. Either the GPS locater wasn't all that accurate, or she hadn't moved since he first located her.

He panted as he pumped his legs uphill, and then stopped at the top. Relief flooded his bones as he spotted Christina sitting on a stone wall. As he made his way toward her, the relief evaporated.

"Christina!"

She turned a blank, pale face to him from her crouched position on the wall. Her eyes were pools of black coffee.

He jogged toward her and kneeled at her feet, running his hands down her arms. "What's wrong? What happened?"

"I..." She closed her mouth and her tongue swept across her lips. She tried again. "My father."

Dread pounded against his temples. Was her father the next victim? "Is he hurt? Did your sister call you?"

Her dark brows collided over her nose. "No."

"What is it, Christina?" He took both of her hands in his. "What happened to your father?"

"N-nothing happened to him." She closed her eyes and her lashes fluttered against her cheeks. "He was here."

He cranked his head around, peering at the empty street, except for a car pulling into a driveway. "Here? Where is he?"

Tilting her head back, her eyelids flew open, and she scanned the sky. "He appeared in front of me, Eric."

He swallowed as a chill crept over his flesh. "Appeared?"

"Like a...an apparition."

He fell back on his heels. Great. Christina was seeing ghosts. "You mean he wasn't physically here?"

"Not physically. He appeared to me. It was him and it wasn't. It was his face and form. I don't know how else to explain it. I've never seen anything like it before. He's never appeared to me like that before."

He liked it better when Christina joked about this stuff. "Did he do or say anything?"

"Not really. No words, but he was warning me."

"Could it have just been your imagination?"

"In a way, it was my imagination, but he willed it. I didn't conjure him up."

"What was the warning?"

"He didn't speak. It was a feeling, a sense."

His breathing slowed down. He could make sense of this. "Obviously, you'd think he was warning you, he and your sister. The warning manifested itself in this vision."

"You're trying to explain it away in practical terms, but it was more than that. His warning chilled me, much more than my sister's words over the phone."

"If someone appeared to me out of thin air, I'd be freaked out, too."

"It was different than that." She uncurled her body and raised her arms to the sky as if trying to bring him back. "It was something about our legacy, our heritage."

"You know that already, Christina. This is your father's coven that's being hunted down, your coven."

She shook her head. "They're coming for me. They must be coming for me."

He took her trembling frame in his arms, to hell with her deception. "We know that. If we didn't know that after the car aiming for you two nights ago, we knew it after the attack on you last night, which is why you shouldn't be wandering the streets by yourself—even if you are a big bad FBI agent with a big bad weapon. I should've never allowed it."

She heaved a sigh and spoke into his shoulder, her words muffled. "That would've gone over real well with me."

"I should've gone with you."

"How'd you find me?"

He reached into his pocket for his phone and held it up. "Remember the GPS trackers?"

"I'm glad we have those, even though I wasn't in any danger from my father."

"Let's get you back to the hotel. You're in no condition to walk back. Your body hasn't stopped shaking since I found you."

He called a taxi and made Christina sit on the wall while they waited. A couple trundled up the sidewalk toward them.

The woman asked, "Is this the right way to Coit Tower?"

Eric pointed ahead. "You'll start seeing signs on that next block. Just keep walking uphill and following the signs."

They thanked him and continued their trek.

A taxi pulled up to the curb and Eric gave him the name of their hotel.

By the time Christina got back to the room, her color had returned to normal and her eyes had lost their glassiness.

Was she losing it? Was the strain of this case too much for her? Too personal? He could relate to all of that.

"I want you to lie down." He pulled the covers down on her bed. "I'll get you some water."

She hooked her finger around the straps of her sandals and pulled them off. She hopped onto the bed—the same bed where he'd made love to her, claimed her again as his own. The same bed where he'd discovered he had a daughter.

He ran a hand across his head while crouching before the fridge. He had all the time in the world to be mad at her for that. Now wasn't the time.

He poured her a glass of water from the bottle and put it on the nightstand. "Drink."

She took little sips of the water and leaned back against the pillows. "I must be in some incredible danger for him to make an appearance like that. I felt such dread when he was communicating with me."

"I thought you said he didn't talk to you. How was he communicating with you?"

She tapped her head. "With my mind."

"Okay, you lost me."

"It's the same way those…others communicate with me."

"The killers."

"Yeah."

"How come this one, I mean, why aren't you getting any feelings from this one?"

"I'm not sure. It doesn't always happen. I just felt the evil at the base of that tree at the crime scene for Nora."

"Have you tried?" He stood by the window, as far from the bed as he could get, and folded his arms across his chest. "I mean really tried?"

"You know I don't do that." She crossed her legs at the ankles and tapped her feet together.

"But you know how. You told me one time your father

tried to give you some tips, and then your mom charged in and put a stop to it all."

"My father has imparted some bits of advice to me."

"You never tried it out?"

"I did, not in any official capacity as an agent investigating a case, but as a silly teenager and a curious college coed."

"And?" He'd uncrossed his arms and braced his hands on the back of a chair. The air hung heavy between them, and he held his breath so as not to disturb the energy.

Christina had stopped tapping her feet. Looking at her palms spread in her lap, she said, "It scared me."

"Because of what you saw? The feelings?" He couldn't imagine Christina afraid of much. Of course, she'd been afraid to tell him about Kendall.

"It's hard to explain. It was like an onslaught of feelings. Vivi always told me for her it was like grasping at wisps of gossamer and if she tugged too hard, the feeling would go away and she'd have to start over. It was nothing like that for me. Once I opened those doors, I had a hard time slamming them shut."

"Maybe your powers are greater than Vivi's. Just like members of your coven are using their powers for evil, you could use yours for incredible good."

She snorted and fell over sideways on the bed, breaking the spell. "I always got the feeling before that you thought my gift was baloney most of the time…not that you weren't supportive because you were."

"Maybe I've had a change of heart these past few days. Obviously, people believe in witchcraft enough to kill over it, to attack law enforcement. They must be fighting over something."

Christina drew her knees to her chest in a fetal position. "I'm not ready to put myself through any of that. Let's solve this case the good, old-fashioned way—good detective work and boots on the ground."

"That's what I do." He dug his finger into his chest.

"We still need to find out why these four particular people were singled out for murder. Okay, they were all members of the same coven, but whoever is committing these murders is not going to be able to track down every member of this coven, especially if they start going into hiding like my sister did."

"Do you think if the cops questioned the victims' families, they would've revealed the coven connection of their family member?"

She answered, "Probably not to an outsider. Maybe the family members didn't make any connection between the murder and the victim's coven activity. The cops didn't know the right questions to ask and hadn't linked the other victims to the same coven."

"But we *do* know the right questions to ask." Christina rolled from the bed and collected the four case folders from the desk. She returned to the bed and sat cross-legged on the edge, the folders stacked in her lap, a legal pad on top of them. She handed him the first folder. "Family members."

"This is Olivia Dearing, the one that doesn't have a connection to the coven."

"That we know of."

"Right." He flipped through the pages. "Her parents live in Vancouver, wealthy, reclusive."

"Is a transcript of the interview there?"

"Yeah. Maybe we should split them up two and two."

"You know what all of these victims do have in common?"

"Hmm?" She didn't look up from her pad of paper.

"They're all only children."

"Really?" She glanced up. "Do you think that's significant?"

"It's a commonality. It's not too unusual for the younger two, but when the older two were born it was less common to be an only child."

She jotted something down on her pad. "I think we should look at everything. It's down on my list."

Thirty minutes passed and Eric dropped the folder and stretched. "I can't believe we're in here working on a Sunday."

She rolled her shoulders. "It's safe."

"Safe? You're not afraid to go outside now, are you?"

"I meant," she said, wagging her finger back and forth between them, "it's safe between us. If we have our work to concentrate on, we can forget the rest of what's hanging over our heads."

He broke his pencil in two and chucked it across the room. "I just don't get why you didn't tell me."

"If you could've walked out on me last night, left the hotel and never looked back, is that what you would've done?"

"And turned my back on my daughter? Never." His jaw tightened. "I resent that you'd even go there with me."

"You turned your back on me two years ago."

"You seem to have a habit of playing fast and loose with the truth."

She gathered her hair into a ponytail and tossed it over one shoulder. "I didn't lie to you back then, Eric."

"Oh, excuse me. I didn't think to ask the woman I was dating and falling in love with if she happened to have a case file on my father."

"What does it matter? It was a fascinating case then and it's a fascinating case now. I didn't tell you about my notes because I was self-conscious about my interest in the case. I'd always been self-conscious about my interest in serial killers. My mom basically accused me of being a freak. I didn't want to hear that from the man I loved."

"Can't you understand how I felt when I found out? It was ten times worse that you'd been hiding it from me, and then Lopez was there suggesting you were planning to write a book. Our relationship felt like a sham."

She looked down at her fingers pleating the bedspread. "It was never a sham. I just felt like it was one of the many coincidences in my life that I happened to wind up on a task force with you. If we hadn't hit it off, if we hadn't fallen in love, that would've been the end of it."

"But we did and we did, and that's when you should've told me about your little obsession, and then it became a pattern because you neglected to tell me about your pregnancy."

She covered her face with her hands. "I've gone over it a million times. I've regretted it a million times, but I can't wave a magic wand and change it."

"I can't wave a magic wand and erase all my feelings of resentment that you kept me from Kendall, and worse, kept her from me."

She shoved one of the files off the bed. "So, we work."

He rubbed the back of his neck where it felt as if every muscle was knotted. "I'm going to get some food, and then I'm going to follow your example and hit the gym. I finished the report for the P.D. and Rich."

She waved at him. "Knock yourself out."

HE DIDN'T QUITE knock himself out, but he got in a good workout, and then walked through the double doors of the gym to the pool where he slipped into the bubbling hot tub.

He adjusted his position so that the jets hit his lower back. Had he really made it so difficult for Christina to tell him about her pregnancy?

He'd made it clear to her that he never wanted kids. Now

that he had one somewhere out in San Miguel, that claim sounded ridiculous and childish. But how was Christina supposed to know he'd do a one-eighty when confronted with the certainty of fatherhood?

He had his fears about his ability to protect a child, and working the kidnapping task force for the Bureau was supposed to put those fears to rest.

Instead Noah Beckett happened. He'd lost that boy, and although the official report deemed that loss a function of FBI policy, his failure had hollowed out his soul.

That's where he was when Christina got pregnant.

Could he blame her for not telling him in that moment? He didn't even know now what his reaction would've been then.

He puffed out a breath and slid farther into the pool of water until it bubbled around his ears.

She kept the secret for two years. If they hadn't been thrown together on this case, how much longer would she have kept the secret?

He submerged his head and sluiced back his hair when he surfaced. He rubbed his eyes and Christina appeared before him, waving her arms.

"I thought you'd gone under for good."

She had her clothes on instead of that sexy black one-piece she'd shimmied into the other night. Must be here for business, not pleasure, but then what did he expect?

He hitched his elbows on the deck of the hot tub and hoisted himself up. "What's up?"

"I got a call from Libby." She held out the phone. "She wants us to come by her shop."

"Isn't it late?" He'd had dinner, alone, put the finishing touches on the report, alone, and had worked out, finishing up here, alone. "It has to be close to ten o'clock."

"She lives behind her shop. She sounded anxious.

There's something she wants to tell us, something she discovered."

"She couldn't tell you over the phone?"

"She was afraid, same with a text. She wants to tell us in person."

He groaned as he rose from the hot tub, steaming water running off his frame. "I was hoping this hot, churning water would wash away my stress and make sleep a little easier tonight."

Her gaze followed his hands as he plucked the wet board shorts away from his body. Even one suggestive look from her could get him hard.

He snatched his towel from the back of a chair and bunched it in front of him as he dabbed his chest and stomach.

"Have you been having trouble sleeping?"

"Yeah, well last night wasn't exactly restful."

"If you hadn't stormed out of my room, we could've..."

"What?" He snapped the towel at his back. "Gone round and around about why you thought it was such a good idea to keep Kendall from me?"

"I could wear a hair shirt."

"I don't want you to keep apologizing, Christina, or even do penance, although you could probably make a hair shirt look good, too."

She clapped. "A joke. I got some humor out of you."

He dropped the towel in the laundry bin. "I was serious."

CHRISTINA PACED BACK and forth in her room, waiting for Eric to shower and dress. That alone was torture—imagining him naked in the shower.

He seemed to be bending a little. Could he understand now why she didn't tell him at the time of the pregnancy? The way he looked after his team had lost that boy, finding out he was going to be a father might've sent him over the edge. He never would've accepted fatherhood at that point in his life.

Could she have told him last year when he resurfaced after South America? Yes. That's when she should've contacted him. She'd messed up big-time.

He tapped on the door between their rooms. "I'm ready."

She opened the door and looked him over from head to toe. "You clean up nicely."

"Maybe we should just take the car tonight since we probably won't have any trouble parking."

"It's Sunday. There are still going to be people out for dinner."

"Yeah, but not as far down as Libby's shop."

"Sure, I'll drive."

They left the hotel and crossed into the parking garage. She pulled into traffic and headed to the Haight-Ashbury district.

There was still a buzz on the street, but Eric had been right. The people and traffic thinned out as they maneuvered toward Libby's bookshop.

Christina found a metered spot on the street about a block from the alley and backed into it.

As they turned up the alley, shuttered windows and dimmed lights greeted them. Even the colored lights that lined the alley were snuffed out.

"Looks like everyone closes up on Sunday night." Eric glanced at his watch.

"I texted her while you were getting dressed to let her know we'd be here shortly."

"Did she text you back?"

Christina pulled her phone from the pocket of her sweater. "No."

"Hope she didn't take off or lock up. If so, I just wasted a bunch of quarters and a good night's sleep."

Christina tried the door handle and it twisted. "She's still here."

She shoved the door open, and the bells announced their arrival to the dark shop.

"Libby?" she called out, and the books and shadowy objects seemed to swallow up her voice.

Eric nudged her inside and closed the door behind them, setting off the bells again into a merry song at odds with the stillness of the store and the looming shelves that seemed to threaten any intruders into their domain.

Eric called out. "Libby?"

"Maybe she's in her apartment in the back."

Christina dove into her purse for her little flashlight and flicked it on. She aimed it in front of her and crept toward the counter.

"Careful. Don't trip." Eric put his hand on her hip.

She lifted the barrier that extended from the counter to the wall. "Her place is behind the counter. Libby? We're here."

Eric stumbled against her. "Where are the damned lights?"

"I have no idea. Maybe they're in the back." She reached out and swept aside the beaded curtain that separated the store from the back area. The beads clacked and swayed.

Christina swept the mini flashlight across the cluttered room, its tiny beam picking out boxes of books and overstuffed chairs with items stacked on top of them.

Eric whistled. "I hope she doesn't live in this room."

The beam of the flashlight wavered at an oblong opening across the room. "Looks like there's another area back there."

"Maybe she went to bed, Christina. You responded too late and she didn't think we were coming."

"Oh, no. She sounded way too agitated to call it a night

before she told us what was on her mind. Besides, she wouldn't have left her shop unlocked."

"I just hope she doesn't have a gun she's going to turn on us when we crash into her bedroom."

"You can stay here if you're scared." Christina picked her way across the room, the flashlight leading the way. She reached the opening into the other room and tripped.

She flung out one hand to grab the doorjamb and dropped her flashlight. "Shoot."

"Are you okay?"

"I tripped over something and dropped the flashlight." She crouched down and splayed her fingers in front of her to feel for the penlight, since its light had gone out.

Instead her fingers got tangled in hair—sticky, wet hair.

Christina's throat tightened and her scream ended in a choked gasp.

Eric's voice boomed behind her. "Found the light switch. Now I just hope Libby doesn't kill us for disturbing her sleep."

Soft light flooded the room and Christina blinked. Then she looked down into Libby's lifeless eyes.

This time she managed the scream.

Chapter Fifteen

Eric almost fell on top of her, his knees knocking into the back of her head. "Christ, the blood."

Christina held her hand, smudged with blood, to her face and glanced down at the slash across Libby's throat.

Eric had drawn his weapon, and the click of the safety resounded in the small room. He stepped over the body, avoiding the spreading pool of blood, and searched the rest of the room and disappeared in the back.

Christina remained stationary next to the body, her knees locked, her eyes dry.

Eric strode back into the room. "Are you okay? Nothing back there but Libby's living quarters and no sign of a break-in."

"I-I'm…" She closed her lips against the sob welling in her throat.

Eric took a giant step back over the body and hovered over Christina. "Someone slashed her throat. There's so much more blood this time, more of what you'd expect unlike the other crime scenes."

She skimmed her nails across the wood floor. "Nothing to soak it up like at the other crime scenes, or maybe he was more careful this time not to get any on himself."

"Did you touch anything?"

"Just, just her hair. I must've tripped over her shoe or

something. When I reached out for my flashlight, I felt her hair instead."

"I'll call the cops. Can you get up? Feeling any shock?"

At the mention of shock, Christina's teeth chattered but she clenched her jaw. They continued to chatter anyway.

She braced her hand—the unbloodied one—against the doorjamb and started to straighten up. She stopped.

One of Libby's hands was extended from her body, blood smudged the tips of her fingers and the wood floor, not a pool here but a pattern. Christina leaned in closer.

Letters.

"Eric!"

He finished his call to 911 and stepped behind her. "What's wrong? Can't stand up?"

He took her arm, but she shook him off and pointed to Libby's bloody fingers. "Look. She wrote something on the floor in her blood."

"I'll be damned." He cranked his head around. "Where's your penlight?"

She scanned the floor and saw the flashlight peeking from beneath the bottom edge of the door. She pinched it with her fingers and pulled it free. "I have it."

Eric crouched beside her as she aimed the light on the letters Libby had scrawled before she died.

Eric read them aloud. "*L-E-G-A-O?* Is that someone's name? Legao?"

"That's not an *O*, it's a *C*, and there's another letter following it."

"*L-E-G-A-C*, and what's the last letter?"

"It's a *Y*. Legacy. She wrote legacy."

"Is that supposed to be someone's name because it would be a lot more useful if she'd written the name of her killer with her dying breath than the word *legacy*."

"Legacy." The tinny smell of Libby's blood overwhelmed

her. She felt steeped in it even though she had just a little of it on her fingers.

She lurched forward, and Eric caught her under the arms and pulled her up and into his arms.

"You're trembling. Come away from the body. The first responders are on the way."

He walked her back into the shop where a colorful array of tarot cards was spread out in a mocking display. The killer didn't have to put a tarot card between Libby's fingers—she'd had them ready for him. Did she read her own death before it happened?

Sirens wailed outside, their din drawing closer and closer.

Afraid to sit down and disturb any evidence, but unable to stand on her own with her knees knocking together, she clung to Eric.

She'd seen death before, had seen dead bodies in all shapes and forms, had even joked with the rest of the cops to keep the darkness at bay, but she'd never discovered a dead body before, the dead body of someone she'd come to meet.

The sirens stopped in front of the shop, and Christina grabbed Eric's shirt with one hand. "Someone didn't want her talking to us. She did know something, Eric."

"Yeah, legacy, whatever the hell that's supposed to mean."

He left her side to meet the paramedics and cops at the door.

Closing her eyes, Christina dragged in a breath of fresh air blowing in from the open door. Then she squared her shoulders and joined Eric talking to the uniforms.

Two hours later she stood at the sink in her hotel room scrubbing the dried blood from her hand—Libby's blood. She'd tried to help them and paid the ultimate price.

Eric wrapped his arms around her waist and pressed his lips against her hair. "I'm sorry you had to see that."

"I've seen my share of dead bodies—some in a lot worse shape than Libby's." She scrubbed harder, like Lady Macbeth.

"This is different. If not a friend, Libby was an acquaintance, someone trying to help us, someone we were supposed to meet."

"You don't remember legacy, do you?"

His puzzled eyes met hers in the mirror. "Am I supposed to?"

"No, I suppose in all my babbling about seeing the vision of my father, the actual context of the communication got lost."

Eric snapped his fingers. "He said something about a legacy, but it didn't make sense to me then and it doesn't make sense to me now."

She let the hot water run over her pink-stained hand. "It has something to do with the bloodline of witches, our inheritance or something. We have legacy in our family because my father is a brujo and passed his gift to me and my sister."

Eric grabbed a hand towel from the rack and shoved it into her midsection. "I think that's as clean as your hands are going to get right now."

She cranked off the water and buried her hands in the towel.

"I wonder," he mused as he made a half circle around her and leaned against the vanity, "if this legacy thing has anything to do with the fact that all the victims were only children."

"It might. I don't know enough about it. Maybe Libby was going to explain it to us."

"Someone must've thought she was going to do more than that if they killed her to stop her from talking to us."

"Now we have to find another source, and I just don't think Nigel is our guy."

"I don't think anyone's going to be our guy or gal once news of Libby's murder gets around. This killer has put out the word."

"That's only if he knows who we're talking to and if he can get to her." She bunched up the towel and tossed it on the floor.

"Her? Do you have someone in mind already?"

"Vivi."

"You can't reach her on her phone because she doesn't get service down there."

"But your brother can find her. He did it before. He can get word to her."

He raised one eyebrow. "Do you suggest we take a trip to Mexico to track her down? I think we'll have a hard time explaining that one to Rich."

"Maybe someone will be willing to meet with us secretly? The sooner we get this madman off the streets, the safer all witches are going to feel."

"I'd be a lot happier if the police can just lift a fingerprint from the crime scene." Eric squeezed past her on his way out of the bathroom. "Sure, it would be great to know what Libby was trying to tell us by writing legacy in her blood, but that's a roundabout way of catching our guy. Knowing his motive helps, but I think we know enough of his motive to know he's involved in the occult community. I want some hard facts leading to his identity."

"You're right." She wedged a shoulder against the window and tipped her head against the glass. "I think I'm too personally involved in this case. It's skewing my focus."

"Yeah, well, you and me both. Given all the connections of this coven to my kidnapping, I'm getting personally involved, too." He dropped on her bed and punched a pillow with his fist. "What are we going to do? Go to Rich and tell him to take us both off this case because of our personal involvement? That's less professional than sticking it out to the bitter end."

"We have to take a few steps back and take a few deep breaths." She traced Libby's name on the window with her fingertip. "It's obvious Libby didn't know her killer or she would've written his name instead."

"Yep." He sat up on the bed and turned the alarm clock to face him. "It's almost two in the morning. Now is not the time to take a fresh look at this case."

"You're right. We have a busy day tomorrow, and the SFPD has another murder on its hands."

Eric slid from the bed and crossed the room. Cupping her face in his hands, he said, "I'm sorry about tonight."

He drew the pad of his thumb across her lips and followed it with a soft kiss. Then he escaped to his own domain, leaving her alone to ponder his statement.

Was he sorry about tonight because they found Libby murdered, or was he sorry that he was leaving her to her cold bed?

The former he had no control over and no reason to be sorry. But the latter? If he wanted her, why didn't he just take her, damn it?

THE NEXT MORNING, Eric had a hard time keeping his eyes off the tall, beautiful FBI agent in the blue pantsuit standing in the corner of the briefing room. He'd seen Christina's casual side all weekend, but he'd always liked this look on her. She was the woman he'd fallen for—professional, sassy, and hard-as-nails. That made the woman she turned into between the sheets all the more exciting.

Looking at her operate on the job with other law enforcement professionals, anyone would think she'd be a tigress in bed—taking charge and calling the shots. Not. At. All.

That's what had thrilled him the first time they were

together. He liked to be in control in the bedroom, and luckily for both of them, Christina liked relinquishing control once she kicked off those stiletto heels. Or sometimes he made her leave them on. Or sometimes he made her…

"Agent Brody can speak to that."

Eric blinked at the roomful of detectives staring at him, and then glanced at the whiteboard. Where were they?

Christina cleared her throat. "That was more my line than Agent Brody's, so I'll pick up that point."

He nodded briskly as if that was his plan all along.

When the meeting ended, Eric remained at the front of the room nursing his coffee and watching the detectives file out. A few of them stopped by to introduce themselves as friends of his brother Sean.

When the last one exited, leaving him alone with Christina, he exhaled. "That went better than I expected."

"Did you think they'd laugh in our faces? We have proof of the connections between three of the victims—Juarez's tattoo, Liz's necklace with the same symbol, and Nora's employment at Kindred Spirits and her self-identification as a witch in this coven."

"And now Libby's death just before she planned to reveal something to us."

"Legacy." Christina circled the word on the white board.

"I emailed the report to Rich."

"Any input?"

"Not before the meeting, but my phone buzzed a few times while I was up here."

"Is that why you spaced out? You were getting a text or call?"

His nostrils flared. *No, that was when I was thinking about laying you out naked on my bed.* "Just tired."

Her dark eyes widened, and a pink flush stained her cheeks. Had she just used some witchcraft to read his mind?

He dug his phone out of his pocket and swiped his thumb

across the display. "Rich did call, but more important, the Dearings called me back."

"Did they leave you a voice mail?"

He tapped his phone to play back the voice mail and put it on speaker. "Agent Brody, this is Mr. Dearing. I'm returning your call. Please call me back on my cell phone."

He left the number and Eric scribbled it on a slip of paper. "Let's go back to that office and return the call."

They staggered through the squad room with their files and bags. Nobody offered to help them, and Rita's eager face was nowhere to be found this morning.

Christina dropped her bag on the floor outside the office and pushed open the door. They moved their baggage into the office, and Eric dropped behind the desk and tossed his cell phone on top of the blotter.

Christina took the seat across from him and propped her high heels up on the corner of the desk. "Make the call."

"Yes, ma'am." He punched in the cell number Mr. Dearing left and put the phone on speaker.

"Hello?"

"Mr. Dearing, this is Agent Brody with the Federal Bureau of Investigations, and I have Agent Sandoval with me. You're on speakerphone."

"What is it you want to know, Agent Brody? I told the police what I could about my daughter. Are you any closer to finding her killer?"

"I think so, but you can help by telling us about Olivia's association with *Los Brujos de Invierno*."

Mr. Dearing choked on the other end of the line. "What does that have to do with anything?"

"Are you denying she was connected with that coven?"

"I—I don't understand."

"Mr. Dearing, we have strong evidence that the three other victims of your daughter's killer were members of *Los Brujos de Invierno*."

Mr. Dearing groaned. "I thought we'd put all that behind us."

"Us? What do you mean?"

"Legacy."

Eric dropped the pencil he'd been toying with, and his
eyes met Christina's, visible above the hand clamped over
her mouth.

"Legacy? What does that mean?"

"It means it's in the blood. More than any other coven,
Los Brujos de Invierno passes power down from one gen-
eration to the next. My wife's father was a brujo. My wife
was an only child, and Olivia was our only child. Were
these other victims only children in their families?"

"They were."

Mr. Dearing stifled a sob.

Eric squeezed his eyes shut. "Do you know why someone would be killing people like your daughter, Mr. Dearing?"

"For the power. For their blood."

Christina hunched across the table, her voice sharp.
"Why this coven, Mr. Dearing? Why *Los Brujos de Invierno?* We heard a rumor it was because they were a force
for evil."

He blew his nose. "It happens, but they could just as well
use their power for good or personal gain. We've also heard
rumors—rumors of lottery winnings and political power.
It's all power, Agent Sandoval—and someone wants it."

Eric twirled the phone toward him. "Who knew about
your daughter's…ah, legacy?"

"I don't know. She was an adult. She didn't live at home.
We didn't know all her friends. She could've innocently
blabbed it to the wrong person. She wasn't a practicing
witch, but she dabbled."

They couldn't get much more out of him, and Eric didn't
have the heart to keep pressing him. The man was breaking

apart over the phone. To have a daughter, an only daughter, taken away from you in such a cruel manner would have to be almost too much to bear.

And now he was a father, the father of a daughter.

When he ended the call, Christina blurted out. "The blood. Do you think he took the blood?"

He raised his eyes. "Huh?"

"At each crime scene, there was less blood than expected from a severed artery. In most cases, the blood spatter experts on the scene put it down to either the killer walking away drenched in blood or the blood soaking into the dirt or carpet. But I think he took it."

"Like bottled it?"

"Either that or he," she wrapped one slender hand around the column of her throat as she said, "drank it."

"Like a vampire?"

"Like someone who wanted the power in their blood. Think about it. The victims had bruises on their necks. They'd been strangled first and then had their throats slit. He incapacitated them first, and then cut into their jugular to create a spurt of blood—legacy."

"It must not be working if he's still killing. He must not be powerful enough. Where's it going to stop for him?"

"When he finds the most powerful member of *Los Brujos de Invierno*."

"He's looking in the wrong place." She tipped back her chair and crossed her arms behind her head. "The most powerful brujos are in Mexico."

"Including your father?"

She thumped the legs of her chair onto the floor, and dropped her hands in her lap. "Exactly."

"Then maybe he'll head to Mexico."

"I hope for Vivi's sake he doesn't."

"Your father's sake, too?"

"My father can take care of himself." She glanced at her

phone. "I'm having a videoconference call with my mom before lunch. D-do you want to join in?"

"Yeah. It's okay? I can, you know, stay out of view."

She flipped up her laptop and positioned it on the desk. "There's no need to do that. Kendall's going to meet you shortly anyway, so she might as well get a look at you now."

"Has Kendall met many…guys in your life?"

Christina's eyes narrowed to slits and a muscle in her jaw twitched. "I haven't introduced Kendall to anyone. There are no guys in my life, never have been since the day she was born."

He dipped his head once. He could get that. From the moment Christina walked into his life five years ago, there'd never been anyone like her for him. Through all his doubts about her motives, for all his trust issues, even now, she was in his blood.

The screen in front of her cast a glow on her face, or maybe that was just motherhood.

"Hi, girly-girl. Hi, Mom."

Her mother's voice filled the small office. "Are you working?"

"Yes, I'm in an office at the police department. The walls are a little thin, so please keep it down." She gestured to him. "I have Eric with me. He wants to meet Kendall."

"Thank God. It's about time."

Eric scooted his chair around the desk. A little dark-haired girl's face filled the screen, her wide eyes so much like Christina's. Soft curls framed her face, and he knew that wavy hair came from him.

"Kendall, this is Eric. He's going to come and visit you when Mommy comes home."

Kendall waved her hand. "Hi."

"Hi, Kendall. What are you holding?" His throat felt tight and he blinked his eyes.

She looked down at the white plush animal in her arms and then held it up so that it filled the monitor. "It's Kitty."

"Is that his name?"

She wiggled the stuffed toy. "Yes."

"Kendall, put Kitty down so we can see you. I'll call Kitty later. Right now I want to see my girly-girl."

She giggled and dropped Kitty to the floor.

"Tell me what you and G-Ma have been doing?"

Christina was able to coax a few more sentences out of Kendall.

Eric was content just to watch his daughter, a mixture of both him and Christina. A miracle.

Kendall grew restless, and Christina's mom placed her on the floor to play with some puzzles.

"Good to see you again, Eric. I'd been warning Christina all along to tell you about Kendall."

"Ma."

"Now I know, and I want to be a part of her life."

"I never doubted you would. I figured you'd get over that nonsense of not wanting kids once you actually had one."

"Ma." Christina rolled her eyes at him.

Her mother barreled on. "Any idea when this case is going to wrap up?"

"Wish we knew. If it drags on much longer, there's no reason why I can't go home for a visit."

"Oh, I saw that friend of your sister's this morning, the one she was with on her way to who knows where."

"He's in San Miguel?"

"When he was here with Vivi, he mentioned he had friends in San Miguel. Probably stuck around to visit them."

"Yeah, he didn't go with her."

"Did you ever get that all cleared up with her?"

"Yes."

"Flighty girl. See what could've happened to you if your father had his way?"

"Yeah, Ma. We're going to have lunch. Can you please put Kendall back on camera?"

Kendall's face popped up again, a little pouty this time saying goodbye to her mother. She said goodbye to him, too, and that just about made his day.

When Christina ended the connection, Eric slumped back in his chair. "Wow. She's a cutie."

"Yeah, she is. She's very loving and friendly."

"Are you trying to say she'll like anyone? Even me?"

"She'll like anyone. She'll love you." She wrapped a strand of hair around one finger. "Did you notice the curls?"

"Oh, yeah. We're going to have fun taming those." The *we* had just slipped out. How hard could parenting be? His number one job as a father was to keep Kendall safe. He could do that.

"Lunch and then back to the grindstone?" She slipped her laptop into her case. "Are you going to call Rich back?"

"I'll call him before we head out to lunch. We should check with the P.D. to see if they can give us anything on Libby, like if half her blood is missing."

"It won't be. He killed her to shut her up, not for her blood."

As SHE SAT across from Eric in the restaurant looking over the menu, she couldn't help humming to herself. That videoconference had gone great.

Eric had been as taken with Kendall as she knew he would be. Did it mean he'd come running back to her arms after he met his daughter? No, but the introduction of father to daughter in person would be a promising start— for all of them.

"Is that supposed to be a song?" He broke off a piece of bread from the loaf in the middle of the table and swiped it across a puddle of olive oil. "Because I don't recognize it at all."

"It's one of those tuneless hums." She pushed away her bread plate. "If I eat any more of this sourdough bread, you're going to have to shoehorn me out of this restaurant."

He tore off another piece. "Good. More for me."

The waitress took their orders, and Christina squeezed some lemon into her ice water. "I think we have a pretty good handle on why these murders are occurring. Now we just need a who."

"It has to be someone who was at that meeting the other night. You can't tell me the coven community is that big. He has to be a member to know who's who and the power of *Los Brujos de Invierno.*"

"If the others know, why wouldn't they give him up?"

"They don't know." He shrugged and took a sip of his soda.

"You'd think they'd be a little more interested in helping us out."

"After what happened to Libby, they're going to be less interested."

Christina asked, "Rich okay with the direction of the investigation?"

"He's not happy with the mumbo jumbo aspect, but he knows we can't ignore it if all the victims have that in common."

With her fingertip, she caught a bead of moisture trailing down the outside of her glass. "Did you tell him about our personal connections to the case?"

"No, but I plan to visit Marie Giardano in the evidence locker this afternoon to ask her a few questions about my kidnapping. She's been there for years, knew my father."

Their food arrived, and Christina picked at her salad. "I meant what I told my mom. If this case drags on any longer and Rich decides to bring in additional agents, I'm going to start heading home on the weekends."

"How do you like San Miguel? It makes more sense to

me that you're living there now that I know about Kendall. I knew something was off about you giving up the city."

"I didn't think I'd like it, but it grows on you."

"That's what my brother Ryan says."

"So he still likes Crestview?"

"He's the chief of police now."

"You Brody boys sure know how to get ahead in law enforcement." She stabbed a piece of lettuce with her fork. "How much of that is due to your father? To making up for past sins, real or imagined?"

Eric balanced his fork on the edge of his plate and laced his fingers beneath his chin. He gazed past her, his green eyes dark and stormy.

She held her breath. Had she gone too far?

He dragged one hand through his hair as his eyes cleared. "A lot."

Then he dug into his food again, and she let out a long steady breath through her nose. "Do you want me to come with you when you see Marie?"

"Sure. I'd rather the SFPD think I'm working on the current case and not dredging up the past." He leveled his fork at her plate. "Are you going eat that shrimp salad or just push it around your plate?"

"I'm not hungry." She shoved the plate toward him. "Do you want it?"

"I hate to see good shrimp go to waste."

He demolished her salad while she checked her messages. Nothing.

"Hey, has Nigel called you since last night?"

Chewing, Eric shook his head. He swallowed and wiped his mouth with a napkin. "He probably skipped town. He publicly acknowledged us at the meeting the other night. He's gotta feel like he has a target on his back."

"Do you think he does?"

"That depends on how much our killer thinks Nigel

knows. If he's truly a hanger-on, maybe our guy doesn't see Nigel as a threat."

"Not like Libby." She grabbed for the check when the waitress placed the tray on the edge of the table. "I'll put this one on my card."

"Then let's head back. I've got a date with Marie."

Forty minutes later when they'd made their way to the evidence room in the basement, Christina did feel as if she had interrupted a date.

The woman behind the cage squealed when she saw Eric step off the elevator. She knocked her glasses from her nose where they swung on a chain around her neck. "If it isn't one of the bodacious Brody boys come to visit an old lady and make her day."

Eric laughed and grabbed the cage, sticking his fingers through the spaces. "That'll be the day when anyone calls you an old lady, Marie."

She clicked her tongue. "You always were more charming than Sean, but that one's been loosening up ever since he started dating that pretty little blonde."

"A teacher, huh? We haven't met her yet."

"Soft as a spring rain on the outside, that one." She thumped her chest with her fist. "But made of steel inside. She'll be good for your brother."

Christina stood in the background, her hands folded in front of her. Should she try to appear as soft as a spring rain so this formidable woman would approve of her, too? That was gonna be hard.

Eric stepped to the side. "I'm sorry. Marie Giardano, this is Christina Sandoval—Agent Sandoval."

Marie stuck her hand out the window of the cage. "I've heard all about Agent Sandoval from that little Rita Griego. You've got a big fan, Agent Sandoval."

Christina shook the older woman's be-ringed hand.

"Please, call me Christina, and Officer Griego seems like a good cop."

"Oh, she is. She'll go far." Marie tapped the side of her head. "I've seen them come and go, and she's got the fire."

Eric leaned on the counter. "I have to confess, Marie, I didn't come down here just to flirt with you."

"That's okay, son. I'll take what I can get, when I can get it." She winked broadly at Christina.

"I'd like to see the old file on my kidnapping."

Marie frowned, biting her lower lip. "You've seen it before, right?"

"I have, but I learned something recently and I want to check it against the information in the file."

Marie hunched forward, her prominent nose almost touching the mesh. "I'll tell you what I told Sean when he came poking around here in the old file. 'I'll give it to you, but don't bother signing out for it.' That way there's no record."

"Why wouldn't I want there to be a record? It's my own kidnapping."

She shook her head. "Don't ask me that, Eric. There was no record that Sean looked over your father's case files, and yet, Dr. Patrick still wound up dead."

Christina's gaze darted toward Eric. What was Marie implying?

Eric spread his hands. "I told Sean at the time, there was no evidence of foul play in the doctor's death."

"No evidence based on the tests they ran during the autopsy, but what about the tests they didn't run?"

"My brother still thinks Dr. Patrick was murdered?"

"Let's just say he thinks the doc was conveniently silenced right before Sean planned to talk to him."

"There's a lot of that going on." Eric slid a glance Christina's way. "Okay, I'm not signing anything. Where's the evidence?"

Marie pulled up a database on her computer and jotted down a set of numbers on a slip of paper.

As Eric reached for the paper, she snatched it out of his fingers. "Get rid of this once you locate the boxes."

"I'll swallow it." He drew a cross over his heart.

She snorted and buzzed them into the cage.

Marie had given them the general direction of the case number, and Christina followed Eric as he plowed through the rows of shelves, stacked with boxes.

He trailed his hand across one row, murmuring numbers, and then stopped and dropped to his haunches. "It's down here."

Christina rolled a stool on wheels next to Eric's crouching form and sat on it. "How much do they keep down here?"

"They keep the case file and some bits of evidence. One of these days, someone's going to transfer all the old stuff to computer, but until they do," he said, dragging a box from the bottom shelf, "it's all right here."

He knocked the lid from the box and reached in. He drew out a thick folder with dog-eared papers peeking from its edges. Dropping it on the floor, he said, "I'm going to give you half of this."

"What am I looking for?"

"You're a detective, aren't you?" He flipped up the silver fasteners and measured out half the papers with his hand. "Look for references to the occult, examine the pictures of the evidence, read my statements."

"Okay, I get it." She nudged his thigh with the toe of her pointed shoe. "If you think your back is going to get any better all hunched over like that, you're crazy. Grab one of these little step stools. I'm sure there's one on every row."

He tucked his sheaf of papers under his arm and rose to his feet. A minute later he returned, wheeling a stool in front of him.

They perused the files, the silence broken by the shuffling of paper, the squeak of the step stools and an occasional sniffle.

Marie greeted people at the cage window, but nobody ventured this far back into the bowels of the evidence lockup.

Christina had done her research on the Phone Book Killer years ago and had even delved into Eric's kidnapping, but she'd never reviewed the case file on it. Eric hadn't been rescued. His kidnappers had released him. Joseph Brody's defenders pegged the kidnapping as a warning to Brody from the Phone Book Killer to back off. The detective's detractors saw it as a ploy by Brody to divert suspicion from him.

She eyed Eric over the top of her file. No wonder he hadn't wanted kids of his own if he suspected his own father might have had him kidnapped.

Running her finger down the page, she skipped a sentence and then backtracked. "I didn't know you were found in Haight-Ashbury."

"Yep. They dropped me off on a street corner, blindfolded."

"Had they been holding you there, too?"

"I have no idea. They drugged me before they released me. I came to in a moving car, wearing a blindfold, and they pushed me out of the car and told me to stand there and not remove my blindfold."

Her hand was trembling when she turned the next page as her heart twisted for the boy Eric had been. She continued scanning the recovery effort, which involved the residents of The Haight coming forward to help the blindfolded boy abandoned on the street corner.

She skimmed the names of the witnesses and froze.

She must've made a noise because Eric looked over and said, "What is it? Find something?"

Her eyes met his above the edge of the paper now crumpled in her hand. "One of the people who came to your aid in the street that night…"

He dropped his file. "Yeah?"

"Liz Fielding."

Chapter Sixteen

Christina had whispered the name but it roared in his ears. The necklace. The necklace Liz was wearing at the time of her murder was the same one he'd seen dangling above him in his captivity.

"It's her, Christina. Liz Fielding was one of my kidnappers." He thrust out his hand. "What else does the report have about her? Did the cops look into her background?"

She handed him the paper with the witness list. "I haven't gotten that far yet. This is just a witness list, and of course her name jumped out at me."

"Jesus." He smoothed out the paper on his thigh. "What are the chances that one of my kidnappers was wearing that necklace and Liz Fielding just happens to show up during my rescue from the street corner?"

"Pretty low, I'd say. Nigel already told us *Los Brujos de Invierno* were involved in your kidnapping. Now it looks like Liz Fielding was directly involved. What about the other victims?"

"Involved in my kidnapping?" He folded the piece of paper and shoved it in his pocket. "The other two women were too young."

"Do you think your kidnapping has anything to do with this current case?"

"I don't think so, Christina, except for the connection

of *Los Brujos.*" He tugged on his earlobe. "But it makes me wonder if the Phone Book Killer was a member of the coven. He carried out the murders and his coven members worked the PR angle for him."

She folded her hands and pinned them between her knees. "If you ever really had any doubts about your father's innocence, this should blast them to bits. Members of *Los Brujos de Invierno* kidnapped you to threaten your father. Joseph Brody had nothing to do with your kidnapping and nothing to do with those murders."

Eric smacked his stack of papers on the floor where they fanned out in perfect symmetry. "Then why did he kill himself? Why did he jump off the Golden Gate Bridge?"

Christina fell to her knees in front of him. Wrapping her arms around his waist, she rested her head against his thudding heart. "I don't know, Eric. I wish I could help you, but I just don't know."

He pressed his cheek against the top of her head, and stroked her hair. "How could a man do that to his family? I would never… I could never…"

She cupped his chin with one hand and looked deep into his eyes. "I know that."

He took possession of her lips in a fierce kiss that nearly tumbled them both to the floor. How could he ever give up on this woman? She understood him as no one ever had before. And he understood her.

A pair of heavy footsteps split them apart, and Eric jerked his head up in time to see Marie poke her head around the end of the shelf.

"Are you two almost done? It's five o'clock, and I draw the line at working overtime—even for a Brody. You can always come back tomorrow, Eric."

"I think we have what we need, Marie." He gestured at the papers scattered on the floor. "We'll clean up."

"I have a few things to do up front." She backed out

of the aisle as if suddenly becoming aware of Christina's disheveled appearance on the floor between his knees.

He blew out a breath when he heard her pull shut the cage window, and then he knelt beside Christina to scoop up the papers on the floor. "You have the interviews with the witnesses?"

She waved a sheath of papers at him. "I took them out of the file already."

"How big is your handbag?"

"Big enough." She rolled them into a tube and stuffed them into her purse.

He reassembled the case file and dropped it into the box. He tipped the box up onto the shelf and shoved it the rest of the way with his knee.

"Look, I know we didn't do much to advance our own case today, but I owe it to my brothers and…and my dad to investigate this further."

"I agree, and I'm glad to help. You always accused me of being obsessed with this case. Now it's paying off." She winked at him in that ridiculous way she had of screwing up the entire side of her face.

"Thanks." He patted her handbag. "Now we can see what lies Liz Fielding told the police."

She slipped her heels back on and preceded him down the row.

"Wait." He grabbed her shoulder and ran his hand down the length of her jacket, which ended halfway across her derriere.

She jumped. "I know you're kinky, but do you really want to finish what we started right here among the dusty boxes of not-quite-cold cases?"

"I was brushing some dirt from your suit jacket."

"Is that what they're calling it these days?"

He pinched her waist and propelled her ahead of him.

When they got to the front of the cage, he gave Marie a hug. "Thanks a million."

She made shooing motions with her hands. "You two get on out of here, and I'll follow you in ten minutes."

Eric started to smile but noticed the crease between Marie's eyebrows. "You're serious."

"Look what happened to Dr. Patrick the last time I let a Brody in here to look at evidence."

"What are you implying, Marie?"

"Little old me? Not a thing." She made a zipping motion across her pursed lips.

When they got into the elevator, Christina raised her brows. "What was all that about?"

"I don't know. At first with all the business about not signing the evidence roster, I just thought she was protecting me. You know, didn't want me getting into trouble for nosing around the evidence locker."

"Maybe she's just superstitious after what happened to Dr. Patrick."

"Maybe."

They made their way up to the office that they'd claimed as their own. Eric swung his laptop case onto the chair and tapped a key on his keyboard to wake up his computer. Two of his desktop folders were open.

"Hello."

Christina swung her own bag over her shoulder. "What?"

"There are two folders open on my desktop that I did not open."

"Are you sure?" She stood behind him and peered over his shoulder.

"Right here." He ran the cursor across the tool tray at the bottom of the screen. "They were opened and then minimized."

"Are you sure you didn't do it?"

"I usually close out everything when I'm done working."

"But you don't password protect your laptop? Isn't that standard FBI protocol?"

"Shh." He held his finger to his lips.

"Anything important in those two folders?"

"Not really. The report I wrote on the case, a few notes. Nothing classified."

She shrugged. "You probably minimized them yourself and then thought they were closed when you left."

"Probably." He shut down the laptop and snapped the lid closed before sliding it into its case.

On their way through the squad room, Rita waved. "Have a good night."

Eric saluted and Christina waved back. "You, too."

Eric ducked his head and whispered in Christina's ear. "I'm going to put in a good word for her with my brother."

"She deserves it."

Christina got behind the wheel and Eric slammed his door. "Dinner tonight? You must be starving after that pathetic lunch of a few bites of lettuce you had today."

"I am starving." She wheeled out of the parking garage, focusing on the road ahead. "Did you mean dinner together or another solitary meal like last night?"

"Together." He'd planned to take it slow with her, but that kiss in the evidence locker had heated things up. If he wanted slow and easy with Christina Sandoval, he'd have to stop being alone with her. He hadn't yet forgiven her for keeping Kendall from him, but that didn't stop him from wanting her in his bed.

CHRISTINA LEANED INTO the mirror and brushed on a little makeup. Then she smiled at herself—like the cat who'd swallowed the canary. She and Eric had a moment in the evidence locker. He needed her just as much as she needed him. And Kendall needed both of her parents.

She slipped into a pair of flats, black to match her skinny

jeans. They were going casual tonight, walking to a place just off Union Square, but casual could come with a hint of sexy, especially if she hoped to get her man back. With that in mind she pulled on a low-cut sweater.

Eric rapped on the door, and she invited him in. He shoved his hands in his back pockets. "Am I underdressed?"

"These are just jeans."

"No, *these* are just jeans." He dipped his chin toward the slightly faded, totally worn-in denim that hugged his powerful thighs.

"Those are guy jeans, and these are girl jeans."

"I'll say."

Her phone on the nightstand rang. "Sorry, have to get that, just in case."

"Do you want me to step out?"

"I have nothing to hide from you, Eric."

"Anymore."

She glanced at the display—blocked number. She punched the button to answer. "Hello?"

"Christina, it's Vivi."

"Everything settle down for you?" She mouthed Vivi's name to Eric.

"Are you okay, Christina?"

"I'm fine. What's up?"

"I got some news from D-Dad today."

"Is he okay?" Christina's voice sharpened despite her differences with her father. She put the phone on speaker.

"I'm not really his. I'm not really your sister, Chrissy."

"What?" She turned to Eric and shrugged.

"My mother was one of those women who wanted a child with a powerful brujo, and she was so desperate to make it so she lied to our…your father about her pregnancy."

Christina winced and dropped her gaze from Eric's. "Are you sure, Vivi? You're more Dad's daughter than I am in so many ways."

"But not the most important way—blood."

The word caused a chill to run through Christina's body. "It doesn't matter, Vivi. Does Dad know?"

"He knows. He's always known."

"Then it really doesn't matter. He's accepted you as his own. You'll always be my sister."

"But it does matter, Chrissy. It matters to you."

"Not a bit."

"Chrissy, you don't get it. You're—legacy."

Christina clutched the phone and sank to the bed.

"Do you know what that means?" Vivi practically shouted the words over the phone.

"I'm an only child of a brujo."

"A very powerful brujo." Vivi sobbed. "Listen to me, Christina. I know who's taking the blood from those others. It all makes sense now."

"Nothing makes sense. You know who the killer is? Why didn't you tell me before?"

"I just figured it out. When Dad told me today that I wasn't his biological daughter, it all fell into place."

"Tell me."

"He'd been so interested in me, and then it all just stopped. He must've known. He must've found out I didn't have Dad's powerful legacy running through me."

Christina's legacy blood ran cold through her veins. "Are you talking about…?"

"Darius. I'm afraid it's Darius."

Christina dropped the phone and covered her mouth. Through a haze she could hear Vivi's voice squawking at her and feel Eric's arm snake around her shoulders.

"What's wrong, Christina? This is good news. This is a lead." He swept the phone from the floor.

Her nails dug into his arm and she choked. "No. No. Didn't you hear my mother? Darius is in San Miguel. He's after Kendall."

Eric's heart slammed against his rib cage. "Wait."

"What's wrong? What's going on?" Vivi's hysterical voice pierced the air.

Eric spoke into the phone. "Christina's mom saw Darius in San…"

Before he could finish his sentence, Vivi started to wail. "Call her, call Linda right now."

Christina was already on the room phone. "I'm calling her now, Vivi."

Eric took a measured breath. Someone had to keep calm here, and although he felt far from it, the job fell to him. "Is there any other reason for Darius to be in San Miguel?"

"None. He just came along with me. Did Christina reach Linda yet?"

Christina dropped the receiver in its cradle. "She's not answering. I just left a message. Vivi, Mom mentioned something about Darius having friends in San Miguel. C-could that be why he's there? Why are you so sure he's the killer?"

"It just makes sense, Chrissy. He was hanging around me in Santa Cruz, but was always going into the city. He's a minor brujo but wants so much more. He wanted to meet Dad, but you know how Dad feels about mentoring."

"That's purely speculation, Vivi." Eric smoothed his hand across Christina's thigh. Her breathing had returned to normal and she seemed to be putting Vivi's claims into perspective.

"He knows so much about *Los Brujos de Invierno*. He knew, he found out I wasn't really Dad's daughter. It's why he dropped me. It's why he came to the city to meet you. The fact that you're an FBI agent must've scared him off, or maybe your friend scared him off."

"What does Dad say?"

"I haven't told him. How do you think he'd feel if I told him I led Darius right to his only granddaughter?"

"Stay right where you are, Vivi, and tell Dad, or better yet, have him call me."

"There's no phone where we are. He's not going to come into town."

"Not even to save his granddaughter?"

"I'll talk to him, Chrissy. I'm so sorry."

"If Darius is who you say he is, he would've found Kendall on his own."

They ended the call and Christina covered her face with her hands. "I wish Mom would call me back. Where could she be?"

"Out to dinner?"

"My mom cooks. She doesn't go out to dinner, especially not when she has Kendall."

"Did you try her cell phone?"

"Yes. I left a message on her answering machine at home, and then her cell phone voice mail."

"I was talking to Vivi when you called your mom. What did you tell her?"

"I just told her to watch out for Darius and not to leave Kendall alone for a second."

"Call her again. Maybe she didn't pick up because she didn't recognize the number." Eric tossed her cell phone at her and crossed his arms, bunching his hands into his biceps.

Christina tried again. "Mom, give me a call as soon as you can, and stay away from Vivi's friend Darius if you see him. Vivi doesn't trust him. I'm going to try your home phone again, too."

She placed the second call and left the same message on her mom's machine. She cradled the phone in her palm, passing it back and forth. "I'm sorry, Eric. I can't go out to dinner now."

"You have to eat something." He reached for the plastic menu on the nightstand. "Let's do room service again."

"Where could she be?"

"We'll give her another hour, and then we'll call the San Miguel P.D. to check on her. Better yet, I'll have my brother the chief call. I'm sure the chief of police for Crestview has some pull with the San Miguel P.D. I'll call him right now."

He tried his cell first and left a message. Then he called the station.

He listened to a recording about calling 911 for an emergency, and then a human voice came on the line. "Crestview Police Department, can I help you?"

"Is Chief Brody in? This is his brother Eric."

"One moment, sir." There was a thirty second pause, and then she came back on the line. "He'll be right with you."

"Thanks."

He waited another few minutes before his brother's voice came over the line. "Hey, Eric. What's up?"

"I need a favor, Ryan."

"No small talk? Must be important. What do you need?"

"Christina's mother lives in San Miguel and she hasn't answered her phone in—hours. She's elderly, and Christina's worried about her."

"Christina? I thought…"

"Don't ask. Can you contact someone over in San Miguel to facilitate this?"

"Sure. Does this mean you and Christina are getting back together?"

"Don't ask. Give the San Miguel P.D. my number and ask them to call me after they do a safety check."

"Sure and don't be a stranger."

"Thanks." He pocketed his phone. "Ryan's on it."

She closed her eyes. "I'm worried. Remember when we met Darius? He wouldn't shake my hand."

"He was pretty wound up that day."

"Maybe he didn't want contact with me. Maybe he was afraid I'd read him."

"Can you do that?"

"Not really, but I'm sure Vivi filled his head with exaggerations of my power."

"So Vivi's not really your sister."

"I guess not. I'm surprised that Dad knew all along and still mentored her. I mean, what would be the point?"

"Maybe," Eric replied as he traced a pattern on the window with his fingertip, "he thought she was his daughter at first and by the time he found out, the blood didn't matter anymore."

"But the blood does matter—it matters to Darius Cole." Christina chewed on a fingernail. "Eric, Libby must've known about me and Vivi. She told us she traced family trees. Darius got the information from her and then killed her when he thought she was going to tell us."

Eric shoved his hands in his pockets to keep them from pummeling the wall. "That must've been him at the coven meeting the other night. We were worried about him seeing us, but he must've been even more worried about us spotting him there."

"I was face-to-face with him. How could I not know?" She clasped her hands to her chest. "His cologne—I smelled it when I climbed the tree overlooking the site of Nora's murder. It's him. Vivi's right."

Someone knocked on the door and called out, "Room service."

Christina dug her hands in her hair and took a spin around the room. "I can't eat. Why hasn't Mom called yet?"

Eric opened the door and ushered in the waiter with the room service cart. After he signed off on the check, he lifted a silver dome from one of the plates, and the smell of roast chicken wafting from the tray didn't make his mouth water.

He clanged the lid back down and took a sip of water instead. "Sit down and eat, Christina."

She stopped her nervous pacing and skewered him with her dark gaze. "Can you?"

He downed the rest of the water and wished for something stronger. When his cell phone buzzed in his pocket, he dropped the glass. He answered and tapped the speaker. "Agent Brody."

"Agent Brody, this is Chief Picard with the San Miguel P.D. Mrs. Sandoval is fine…"

Christina released a noisy sigh and sagged against the credenza.

"But was tied up and—the little girl is gone."

Chapter Seventeen

A fury, hot and potent, burned in Eric's chest and he slammed his fist against the wall as Christina sank to the floor.

The chief continued, and Eric had to close his eyes to focus on his words. "Mrs. Sandoval didn't see her attacker. He came at her from behind and knocked her over the head. When she came to, she was tied up and her granddaughter was gone. My officers are canvasing the area and we have our crime scene techs on the way for fingerprinting."

Eric exchanged more information with Chief Picard, giving him Darius Cole as a possible suspect. The chief assured him they'd have the SFPD check out Cole's apartment in the city. When he hung up, he joined Christina on the floor.

She sobbed against his chest. "He's not going to be waiting for the police at his apartment. He has our little girl. He's going to take her blood, just like the others. She's third-generation legacy of one of the most powerful brujos in the coven."

And a second-generation victim of kidnapping. He'd failed Noah Beckett, and now he'd failed Kendall. He didn't deserve to be a father.

Christina clung to him. "We have to find Cole. We have

to save Kendall. You were right. It's all about power and he wants to take hers."

His heart thundered in his chest. He'd just found his daughter, and he wasn't about to let some brujo-wannabe steal her away from him.

Adrenaline surged through his body and he rose to his feet, bringing Christina with him. He placed his hands on her shoulders and gave her a little shake, as much for his benefit as for hers. "Think. What does he want with Kendall?"

She sniffled, but her jaw formed a hard line. "He wants her blood. He wants the power that a third-generation legacy will give him."

He released her and drew his hand across his mouth. "The other legacy victims—Olivia, Juarez, Liz and Nora— they weren't enough for him. He was determined to get the blood of the most powerful brujo in that coven—your father."

"Right. He thought he'd start with Vivi, and then found out about me. Maybe he figured the half-diluted blood of Octavio Sandoval was good enough, but when he discovered that I was an only child and that I had an only child, he wanted to improve his chances."

"How else could he improve his chances? He'll want to make sure this time."

"By following the old rituals." She dashed a tear from her cheek. "He obviously knows more about this stuff than I do."

With his fingertips buzzing, he grabbed Christina again. "And where's the best place to perform those ancient rituals and when?"

Her eyes widened. "The old union hall in The Haight— at the witching hour."

THE HAIGHT-ASHBURY DISTRICT—the event that marked his life forever began here and it would end here.

Christina parked the car down the block from the union hall. They took side streets so they could approach the old building from the back. A few homeless people stirred in their makeshift beds in doorways and on city benches, but nobody disturbed them.

A lone car huddled against the chain-link fence that wound its way behind the union hall property. Had that been where Darius parked his car the night he attacked Christina?

She must've had the same thought as she jerked her thumb at the vehicle.

Eric slipped wire cutters from his jacket and quickly pinched a succession of links on the fence to create a hole. He held up his hand to Christina as he crawled through first.

She joined him on the other side, and he pulled her against the wall of the building where Uma had sent her looking for the restroom.

They flattened themselves against the building and edged around the corner. The high windows of the union hall were dark, but Eric's nostrils flared at the smell of smoke.

Grabbing his belt loop, Christina pressed her lips to his ear. "I smell fire."

He nodded and scoped out the building.

He hadn't called in the cops. He couldn't afford to take orders from anyone this time, couldn't afford to lose his daughter like he'd lost Noah. He'd do this his way.

Drawing his weapon, he hunched forward and darted from tree to planter across the quad, Christina hot on his heels.

They confronted the double doors into the hall, firmly closed. Eric pressed his hand against the cool metal of the door, but it didn't budge.

He stepped back and surveyed the building. A tree nestled against the building, its branches lookout posts into the high windows that ringed the hall.

He nudged Christina and pointed up at the tree.

She got it. She knew what they had to do. No waiting around. No surrounding the building waiting for law enforcement. No talking to the kidnapper as he held Noah… Kendall.

Eric boosted Christina into the tree first. She held on to a branch and walked up the trunk, sure-footed in her running shoes.

Holstering his gun, he followed her into the reaches of the tree until she stopped right above him. She cupped her hand around her mouth and hissed down at him, "Fire."

He pulled himself up beside her and peered through the murky window. A light flickered on the floor of the hall, and then he saw a dark shape emerge from the front of the room—a man carrying a child.

Drawing his weapon, he nodded to Christina. "I'm going in. We can't wait."

He wouldn't wait.

He bent his leg at the knee and then thrust his foot forward, his heavy motorcycle boot crashing through the window. He dropped through the jagged glass, grabbing the cord from the blinds and swinging into the building like a clumsy Tarzan.

The man inside the hall yelled and stumbled back, but not far enough.

By the time Eric staggered to his feet, shaking broken glass from his hair, Darius Cole had regained his footing and had a limp Kendall tucked beneath one arm—a knife to her throat.

Christina screamed as she hit the wall, dropping the cord and falling to her knees. "Leave my daughter alone."

Cole growled, his dark mouth a slash across his pale face. "How did you find me here?"

Jumping up, Christina sneered. "It wasn't through witch-craft. Where else would you go to perform your whacked-out ritual?"

"Whacked-out ritual?" Cole spit into the fire. "You would say that—you who have everything and chose to throw it all away."

At least the man's forward progress toward the fire with Kendall had halted.

Eric waved his gun. "Why those victims?"

"You're here." Cole eyed the weapon. "You must know about legacy. Those others were second-generation legacy, and that's what saved you in the end, Christina."

"You attacked me here?" She'd dropped her gun in the fall through the window and glanced at it on the floor.

"My friend, Denise, helped me lure you outside."

"You mean Uma?"

"You didn't expect her to tell you her real name, did you?"

Eric took a step toward the fire. "And the car? Was that you, too?"

"That was just a warning, a way to frighten you away from the case. What good would your blood have done me spilling out in the street?"

"W-when did you figure out my daughter was third gen-eration legacy?"

"When I broke into that stupid old woman's store and stole her research on the coven families. Vivi wasn't even related to Octavio Sandoval."

Eric shuffled closer until the heat from the flame warmed his face. "What do you hope to accomplish from killing a child and drinking her blood?"

Christina let out a whimper.

"You have no idea, do you, Agent Brody? You have no clue about the power *Los Brujos de Invierno* have. It might surprise you to learn about this city's rich and powerful having that blood running through their veins." He lifted Kendall with one arm, the knife poised above her. "This blood."

"If you touch her with that knife, I'll shoot you where you stand."

"You can't." The knife gleamed in the firelight. "I already have the blood. It's coursing through me. You can't harm me. Now drop the weapon or I slit her throat right now." He pressed the silver blade to Kendall's neck.

Christina shouted, "Eric!"

Did she want him to drop it or not? Didn't matter.

Cole was insane, and he thought he was invincible—a dangerous combination. There would be no reasoning with him. No talking.

Eric's muscles coiled. He held out his gun and dropped it. As soon as Cole moved the knife to his side, Eric jumped across the fire. He tackled Cole, who raised his knife once again.

Eric ripped Kendall from the madman's grasp just as the blade came down, grazing Eric's arm.

Christina swooped in and yanked Kendall away from the two bodies grappling on the floor, their hands warring for the knife.

"Christina, my weapon!"

With a final burst of energy, Cole threw him off and then rolled into the fire. It caught his hair first, fueled by the oil he used to slick it back.

He wailed and then began chanting gibberish.

Next the flames leaped up to the cloth hanging from the table. Whatever Cole had in those containers exploded. And his chanting continued.

"Get her out! Get Kendall out!" Eric stumbled to his feet, his gaze darting around the room for something to use on the fire.

Another small explosion rocked the room, and Christina

called from the double doors, "Get out, Eric. The whole room's going up in flames."

He choked and ran for the fresh air. Before following Christina outside, he glanced over his shoulder at Darius Cole writhing in the fire, his mouth still moving.

He slammed the door.

They ran across the quad and Eric pulled out his cell phone to call 911.

They clambered through the hole in the fence and ran back toward the street. Christina had Kendall clasped to her chest.

When they stopped at the corner, Eric held out his arms for Kendall. "Is she okay? Did that maniac hurt her?"

"I—I think she's just drugged, and she's coming out of it." She transferred Kendal from her arms to his. "You did it, Eric. You saved our daughter—your daughter."

He looked down into Kendall's sweet, innocent face and knew he'd never leave her, never let any harm come to her. He was a father, and he'd saved himself, too.

Epilogue

Kendall pointed to the yellow daffodils his brother's girl-friend, Elise, had arranged in a vase on the table. "What's that?"

Christina tugged one of Kendall's curls. "They're flowers, silly."

Then Kendall touched her finger to Eric's nose. "What's that?"

"Oh, now I know you're just being goofy."

Elise, sitting cross-legged on the floor, picked up a picture book. "Do you want to look at the book, Kendall?"

Kendall slid from his lap and trotted over to Elise.

His brother Sean smiled at the picture of Elise pulling Kendall into her lap and opening the book. "Elise can keep her occupied for hours. She's great with kids."

Christina tapped Sean on the head as she walked behind him. "Are you trying to tell us something?"

Sean swatted at her hand. "Some of us actually plan to get married before having kids."

"Oh?" Christina widened her eyes. "*Now* are you trying to tell us something?"

"One thing at a time." Sean stretched his long legs in front of him. "We're just enjoying our time away here in San Diego."

Eric asked, "How many more weeks are you out?"

"Haven't decided yet, why?"

"I was going to have you put in a word for Officer Griego to make detective, but I heard she was involved in a shoot-out just when we were wrapping up there."

"I heard that, but she's going to be okay. I'll talk to her about it when she's back on duty and I'm back from my leave." Sean crossed his arms behind his head. "So, you really think the Phone Book Killer was somehow involved in all this witchcraft stuff?"

"I don't know for sure, but my kidnappers definitely were."

"Or at least one of them." Sean wagged his finger at him. "Don't jump to conclusions."

"Like you did when Dr. Patrick wound up dead?"

Sean's finger moved to his lips as he glanced at Elise reading the story to Kendall. "She's the one who found him."

"Well, if you're interested in finding out more," he said, kicking a box at his feet, "I have Christina's notes on Dad's case."

Sean eyed the box stuffed with papers. "You hauled that all the way down to San Diego?"

"I can haul it back to Christina's place in San Miguel, if you want." He cleared his throat. "I'll be joining her there as soon as I finish up my next assignment, which is going to take me back to D.C. for a few months."

"You'd be better off giving those notes to Ryan."

"Why's that? He was never much interested in the old man's case—too young to remember much of it." Christina sat next to him on the couch and he grabbed her hand and pulled it into his lap.

"I guess Ryan didn't tell you."

"Uh-oh. Tell me what?"

"Some true crime writer contacted him about doing a book on Dad, and I think he agreed."

Christina squeezed his hand. "It must be that one we saw on TV, the one Ray told us about. Are you okay with that?"

Eric blew out a breath. "Maybe it's time."

"Maybe it's time I get to know my niece a little." Sean pushed up from his chair and joined Elise and Kendall on the floor.

"We can give this stuff to Ryan." She shoved the box with the toe of her shoe. "You're sure you're okay with a book?"

He cupped the side of her face with one hand. "I'm okay with a lot of things."

"I'll never keep anything from you again, Eric. I was so foolish."

He kissed her mouth and drew his tongue across her lips. "Very foolish, and you're going to have to pay in oh, so many ways."

Her dark eyes lit up. "I'll do anything to make it up to you…anything your heart desires."

Her low, purring voice sent a shaft of lust straight to his core. "When is Kendall's nap time again?"

She chuckled and nuzzled his ear. "Looks like Kendall has bewitched her Uncle Sean."

He slipped his hands beneath her shirt, spanning her bare back. "Her mother bewitched me long ago—and she didn't even need her special powers to do it."

* * * * *

Look for more books in Carol Ericson's
BRODY LAW *miniseries later in 2014.*
You can find them wherever
Harlequin Intrigue books are sold!

INTRIGUE

Available May 20, 2014

#1497 RESCUE AT CARDWELL RANCH

Cardwell Cousins • by B.J. Daniels

When Texas P.I. Hayes Cardwell arrived for his brother's wedding, he didn't expect to play hero. But after he saved McKenzie Sheldon from abduction, he couldn't get her out of his mind and heart. Can he protect her from a killer hiding in plain sight who's about to spring a final trap?

#1498 TRACELESS

Corcoran Team • by HelenKay Dimon

Corcoran Team leader Connor Bowen is desperate to locate his kidnapped wife, Jana, who walked out on him seven months ago. Can Connor get to her—and reconcile—before time runs out?

#1499 THE RENEGADE RANCHER

Texas Family Reckoning • by Angi Morgan

Nearly broke, Lindsey Cook turns to rancher Brian Sloane for help. But will Brian uncover the motive and unmask the killer before he annihilates the entire Cook family?

#1500 GROOM UNDER FIRE

Shotgun Weddings • by Lisa Childs

When Tanya Chesterfield's groom is kidnapped, she marries her bodyguard so she can meet the terms of her grandfather's will, collect her inheritance and pay the ransom. But there's no ransom demand made—only attempts on her life and her new husband's life.

#1501 SHATTERED

The Rescuers • by Alice Sharpe

It's up to adversaries-turned-lovers Nate Matthews and Sarah Donovan to disrupt a sinister terrorism plot aimed at striking fear in the hearts of every person in the country....

#1502 THE DEFENDER

by Adrienne Giordano

Sparks fly when sassy Chicago defense attorney Penny Hennings teams up with FBI agent Russ Voight to catch a murderer. But will Penny sacrifice both their lives to get justice? _____

HICNM0514

REQUEST YOUR FREE BOOKS!
2 FREE NOVELS PLUS 2 FREE GIFTS!

⊬HARLEQUIN

INTRIGUE

BREATHTAKING ROMANTIC SUSPENSE

YES! Please send me 2 FREE Harlequin Intrigue® novels and my 2 FREE gifts (gifts are worth about $10). After receiving them, if I don't wish to receive any more books, I can return the shipping statement marked "cancel." If I don't cancel, I will receive 6 brand-new novels every month and be billed just $4.74 per book in the U.S. or $5.24 per book in Canada. That's a savings of at least 14% off the cover price! It's quite a bargain! Shipping and handling is just 50¢ per book in the U.S. and 75¢ per book in Canada.* I understand that accepting the 2 free books and gifts places me under no obligation to buy anything. I can always return a shipment and cancel at any time. Even if I never buy another book, the two free books and gifts are mine to keep forever.

182/382 HDN F42N

Name _____ (PLEASE PRINT)

Address _____ Apt. #

City _____ State/Prov. _____ Zip/Postal Code

Signature (if under 18, a parent or guardian must sign)

Mail to the **Harlequin® Reader Service:**
IN U.S.A.: P.O. Box 1867, Buffalo, NY 14240-1867
IN CANADA: P.O. Box 609, Fort Erie, Ontario L2A 5X3

**Are you a subscriber to Harlequin Intrigue books
and want to receive the larger-print edition?
Call 1-800-873-8635 or visit www.ReaderService.com.**

* Terms and prices subject to change without notice. Prices do not include applicable taxes. Sales tax applicable in N.Y. Canadian residents will be charged applicable taxes. Offer not valid in Quebec. This offer is limited to one order per household. Not valid for current subscribers to Harlequin Intrigue books. All orders subject to credit approval. Credit or debit balances in a customer's account(s) may be offset by any other outstanding balance owed by or to the customer. Please allow 4 to 6 weeks for delivery. Offer available while quantities last.

Your Privacy—The Harlequin® Reader Service is committed to protecting your privacy. Our Privacy Policy is available online at www.ReaderService.com or upon request from the Harlequin Reader Service.

We make a portion of our mailing list available to reputable third parties that offer products we believe may interest you. If you prefer that we not exchange your name with third parties, or if you wish to clarify or modify your communication preferences, please visit us at www.ReaderService.com/consumerschoice or write to us at Harlequin Reader Service Preference Service, P.O. Box 9062, Buffalo, NY 14269. Include your complete name and address.

HI13R

SPECIAL EXCERPT FROM

 HARLEQUIN®

I N T R I G U E

Read on for a sneak peek of
RESCUE AT CARDWELL RANCH
by NEW YORK TIMES *bestselling author*

B.J. Daniels
Part of the **Cardwell Cousins** *series*

When Hayes Cardwell arrived in Big Sky, Montana, for his brother's wedding, the Texas P.I. didn't expect to play hero. But ever since he saved her from a brutal abductor, he can't get McKenzie Sheldon out of his mind and heart.

Hayes stepped out into the cool night air and took a deep breath of Montana. The night was dark, and yet he could still see the outline of the mountains that surrounded the valley.

Maybe he would drive on up the canyon tonight after all, he thought. It was such a beautiful June night, and he didn't feel as tired as he had earlier. He'd eat the sandwich on his way and—

As he started toward his rented SUV parked by itself in the large lot, he saw a man toss what looked like a bright-colored shoe into his trunk before struggling to pick up a woman from the pavement between a large, dark car and a lighter-colored SUV. Both were parked some distance away from his vehicle in an unlit part of the lot.

Had the woman fallen? Was she hurt?

As the man lifted the woman, Hayes realized that the man was about to put her into the trunk of the car.

What the hell?

"Hey!" he yelled.

The man turned in surprise. Hayes only got a fleeting impression of the man, since he was wearing a baseball cap pulled low and his face was in shadow in the dark part of the lot.

"Hey!" Hayes yelled again as he dropped his groceries. The wine hit the pavement and exploded, but Hayes paid no attention as he raced toward the man.

HIEXP69764

The man seemed to panic, stumbling over a bag of groceries on the ground under him. He fell to one knee and dropped the woman again to the pavement. Struggling to his feet, he left the woman where she was and rushed around to the driver's side of the car.

As Hayes sprinted toward the injured woman, the man leaped behind the wheel, started the car and sped off.

Hayes tried to get a license plate, but it was too dark. He rushed to the woman on the ground. She hadn't moved. As he dropped to his knees next to her, the car roared out of the grocery parking lot and disappeared down the highway. He'd only gotten an impression of the make of the vehicle and even less of a description of the man.

As dark as it was, though, he could see that the woman was bleeding from a cut on the side of her face. He felt for a pulse, then dug out his cell phone and called for the police and an ambulance.

Waiting for 911 to answer, he noticed that the woman was missing one of her bright red high-heeled shoes. The operator answered and he quickly gave her the information. As he disconnected he looked down to see that the woman's eyes had opened. A sea of blue-green peered up at him. He felt a small chill ripple through him before he found his voice. "You're going to be all right. You're safe now."

The eyes blinked then closed.

Can he protect her from a danger that's much closer than they think…a killer hiding in plain sight who's about to spring a final trap?

Find out what happens next in
RESCUE AT CARDWELL RANCH
by NEW YORK TIMES *bestselling author B.J. Daniels,*
available June 2014, only from Harlequin® Intrigue®.